DEATH WITH A SMILE

Jethro approached her, eyes greedy, grime-rimmed mouth working in lewd parody of tender kisses. Well, the boys had voted to kill Lone Wolf and rape her, had they? Not all the votes were in, they would soon find out. Moving carefully, the White Squaw slid her right hand into the draw-string puckered top of her small beaded bag. The time had come for her to cast her vote.

She did it with her little .38 Smith and Wesson Baby Russian.

In an instant the slug split the point of Jethro's chin and deflected backward to lodge in the root of his tongue.

Then Rebecca walked toward his partner—the next victim. As she drew nearer she deftly snapped open the tilt-top frame of her Baby Russian and ejected the spent cartridges. Competently she fed new fodder to the reliable little Smith, her gaze never leaving Jo-Ray.

Jo-Ray's pallor increased at his sudden knowledge. Oh, what a terrible mistake he and his brother had made. Eyes wide with fear, body robbed of all energy, he raised his hands in pitiful appeal.

"W-what are you gonna do now?"

Rebecca gave him a radiant smile as she cocked the Baby Russian and centered its muzzle on the middle of Jo-Ray's forehead.

"Kill you."

WHITE SQUAW
Zebra's Adult Western Series
by E.J. Hunter

#1: SIOUX WILDFIRE   (1205, $2.50)

#2: BOOMTOWN BUST   (1286, $2.50)

#3: VIRGIN TERRITORY   (1314, $2.50)

#4: HOT TEXAS TAIL   (1359, $2.50)

#5: BUCKSKIN BOMBSHELL   (1410, $2.50)

#6: DAKOTA SQUEEZE   (1479, $2.50)

#7: ABILENE TIGHT SPOT   (1562, $2.50)

#8: HORN OF PLENTY   (1649, $2.50)

#9: TWIN PEAKS—OR BUST   (1746, $2.50)

*Available wherever paperbacks are sold, or order direct from the
Publisher. Send cover price plus 50¢ per copy for mailing and
handling to Zebra Books, Dept. 1831, 475 Park Avenue South,
New York, N.Y. 10016. DO NOT SEND CASH.*

#10 SOLID AS A ROCK

BY E.J. HUNTER

ZEBRA BOOKS
KENSINGTON PUBLISHING CORP.

Special acknowledgements to Mark K. Roberts

ZEBRA BOOKS

are published by

Kensington Publishing Corp.
475 Park Avenue South
New York, NY 10016

First printing: May 1986

Printed in the United States of America

This volume is dedicated to a tough and independent lady,
PATRICIA CUMMINS, with thanks and respect.

EJH

"*At first, white women were taken as playthings* [novelties]. *They made good slaves. All worked hard, some lived a long time. Babies born to them were considered part of the people. It was about the time of the whites big war [1860–65] that anyone thought of keeping them* [new captives] *for wives.*"

—Red Hand
of the Oglala

"*The camp women, some of them white, came down to the bank to greet us. What a pitiful sight these captives made. It wrung at our hearts.*"

—Reynard Toussant
The *Voyaguers*

Chapter 1

They rode through a riot of color. Fall had used a broad brush to give its signature to the mountain glades of Idaho and northeastern Oregon. Silently, save for the occasional jingle of curb chains and nicker of horses, the fifteen men advanced toward their goal. Gray smudges of alderwood smoke stained the pale blue of the sky ahead. Lew Gorce, the leader, tensed at the sight of them. Silently, he signaled for his men to rein in.

"Not too far now," he informed them in a hushed voice.

"We got the Salmon River between us an' them villages," Clem Dye remarked.

"An' them Palouse horses, too," Sy Burton added.

"There's a ford ahead," Gorce informed his men. "Another two hours will see us in position."

"You mind goin' over again how we're gonna take them horses, get 'em across the river and away without bein' cut to pieces by the Nez Percés?"

"Sure, Niel," Gorce responded.

For a moment he studied this trio. Of the three, Sy Burton had to be the most reliable. At thirty—his own age, Lew acknowledged with a touch of regret for days gone by—Sy had ridden the owl hoot trail for eleven years. Short and stocky, he had the typical temper of a little man in a world of bigger souls. His icy gray eyes had the cast of a calm and competent killer, the scars in his brows, at the corners of his eyes, and on his upper lip illustrated his life as a brawler. He'd probably been using his fists since the age of eight or so. A good gun . . . but unpredictable in what should be calmer moments. Lew's eyes shifted to Niel Thorne.

City kid. It was written all over the narrow, pallid face. He'd been in the west only two years, since his release from the New York State Detention Home for Wayward Boys. Hell, Lew thought with mild irritation, at nineteen Niel didn't even have peach fuzz on his soft, freckled rat face. A wisp of a smile touched Lew's thin lips, exposing large, horsey teeth as he examined Clem Dye.

Although four years Lew's junior, Clem seemed the most even-tempered of the three. His pasty white complexion—a condition consistent with his bright carroty hair—and high-pitched voice caused some to commit the error of thinking Clem a sissy. Over the past four years, six men who made public statements to that effect learned of their grave mistake in a flurry of gunshots. In each case, when the smoke cleared, the imprudent gentleman left behind only a memory along with a grieving widow and sobbing children. Even-tempered Clem couldn't abide being called a sissy. Lew gathered his straying thoughts and summarized his plan.

"There's fifteen of us. Once the herd is started across the Salmon, six men can handle 'em. The other nine will hold back and delay any Injuns who decide to come after us. When the horses are on this side, we pull back in relays, keepin' the savages at bay. Then a quick dash and

10

across the river." Lew shrugged. "After that, it's easy. Into Oregon and south to Pendleton."

"And all that money," Sy said dreamily.

"Right. Now, let's move out." Lew took the lead.

Silver Eel had known twelve summers. In his short life, he had enjoyed frolicking in the snows of *Enim*, playing the stickball game in *Etaiyam*, swimming in *Taiyam*, and grappling in the run-hit-knock-around game nearly any season. Most of all, he loved to watch over the beautiful horses of the *Cho-pun-nish*. Long ago, black-robed white men from the north had given his people a funny name, *Nez Percé*, which meant pierced noses. But hardly anyone did that any more, though the name stuck. The spotted-rump ponies were the true wealth of the *Cho-pun-nish*. For two summers now, Silver Eel had been privileged to join the older boys in guarding the herd of their Salmon River band.

Even their headman, dignified old *Peopeo Kiskiak Hihi*, had praised Silver Eel for his diligence in caring for the magnificent brutes. It made him puff out his chest and walk with the swagger of a warrior. Now, with the coming of the Moon of *Aiakal pikunme* in the season of *Sahnim*, his work had become more difficult.

A summer of grazing had left the pastures close to the clan villages sparse, dry, and brown. The herd had been moved far down the banks of the Salmon River, where the deep, placid pools lay in which the salmon spawned in this Moon named for that event. So far in fact—more than a half-day's ride—that the boys got to sleep out with the horses. Silver Eel liked that even more. His stomach rumbled and reminded him that it was nearly midday.

11

"Ho! Spotted Salmon," Silver Eel called to his friend close by. "My belly aches for lack of food. Let's catch a bull salmon and roast him on alderwood."

Spotted Salmon, lean and berry-brown, looked at his chubby companion and his black eyes glistened with mischief. "You think too much of eating, Silver Eel. Already your belly hangs out over your loincloth, like our headman, White Goose."

"You're too skinny!" the younger boy fired back.

"A warrior's supposed to be thin and wiry," Spotted Salmon retorted.

Silver Eel patted the round, bronze melon of his abdomen. "My father says I'll lose this when I start to grow. It's not fair that you have one summer more than I. *I'll* get thin, you wait and see."

Spotted Salmon hooted with derisive laughter, though he did rise and start off through the waist-high grass toward a pool favored by the boys for catching salmon for their meals. Silver Eel trotted along until he caught up. Side by side, they passed the cooking place and picked up two long poles with braided Indian hemp-fiber nets at one end. Coated with thick layers of plentiful pitch, they served as excellent fishing rods. The boys took them along to the river. Behind them the noises of the grazing camp continued.

Some of the youths set about preparing their own meals. Others took turns at watching the aimlessly moving spotted-rump ponies as they munched their way through the grass, heads down, jaws working in placid rhythm. Silver Eel spotted a big green-backed salmon and swished his net downward.

An enormous weight, like a boulder or a newborn colt, tugged on his arms, and he grounded the butt of his dip net to gain more leverage.

"Haul him in, Silver Eel!" Spotted Salmon shouted in shrill encouragement. "Pull harder. Don't let him get away."

"I'm trying," the twelve-year-old snapped back impatiently. *He* knew how to land a salmon. He didn't need Spotted Salmon's advice.

Suddenly the net whipped over his head and the slippery burden it bore flopped and floundered on the bank. He'd landed the first catch! Silver Eel swelled with pride. He stabbed a short, grubby thumb at his bare chest.

"*I* have our meal. Now it's up to *you* to catch something for the other boys."

"You have to help," Spotted Salmon challenged, a bit of a pout shaping on his full, well-formed lips.

Both boys bent low to swing their nets after chosen prey.

That put them out of sight when the first shots blasted through the quiet of the glade.

"What's that?" Silver Eel asked with a tremble in his voice.

Spotted Salmon peeked over the ridge of the bank. Large, fully clothed figures swarmed into the clearing. They carried the shooting sticks of the white man, and their pale faces identified them positively. Spotted Salmon slid back and whispered close to his friend's ear.

"White men. They have come to steal our horses."

Silver Eel reared up, one fist clinched around his net pole. "They won't get away with this."

His companion reached out and restrained the hot-headed lad. "Stay down. They can't see us here. There's too many of them. I counted three hands of men. They all have guns. We must wait and see what is best to do."

"But our friends . . . ?" Silver Eel protested feebly.

Tears formed in thirteen-year-old Spotted Salmon's eyes. "For them it is too late."

"Like shootin' fish in a barrel!" Beauregarde Bettles shouted to Sy Burton as he triggered off another round.

Brown-skinned youngsters ran every which way as the rustlers swarmed out of the trees and descended on the grazing herd of Nez Percé horses. Three of them fell dead before a shout of alarm could be given. Beau Bettles took aim at another, a sick grin of blood lust on his lips at the moment the older lads reacted.

Two *Cho-pun-nish* boys grabbed their sturdy hunting bows and nocked arrows. The long, wicked bone points, barbed with incised bits of shell, drew to the back, resting against the dip, above the grip, then leaped away through the clear air. Bettles lost his shot as one of the vicious projectiles buried deep in his right thigh.

Instinctively, he swatted at the stinging pain, then howled in agony as he agitated the shaft and its keen-edged point savaged more flesh. The other bolt lodged in the right side of his mount's neck. A horrible scream of agony came from the wounded beast, and it gathered its muscles for a mighty bound.

Weakened by shock, Beau went sailing from the saddle as his horse bolted into the air and began to crow-hop. The heavyset outlaw lay on his back, winded, eyes glazed in pain as he watched the mad swirl of legs around him. The flankers had closed in and jumped the Palouse horses into startled motion.

Horror paralyzed Beauregarde Bettles as the surging horses chose to run in his direction. Beau shrieked in hysteria as the flying hoofs began to pound him into a mud-caked red jelly.

"Shoot! Shoot!" Lew Gorce bellowed. "The little buggers are getting away."

More arrows made wasp sounds in the air around Lew's head. He swung his Smith and Wesson .44 Russian toward the courageous Nez Percé boys and let fly a round. His slug smacked solidly into the belly of one fourteen-year-old. The impact upset the lad and dumped him in a glowing cookfire.

Pitiful yelps of agony came from the boy as the fire tormented him until he died of internal bleeding, caused by the bullet wound. His friend sought instant revenge.

An arrow point shattered against the wide, thick leather of Lew's cartridge belt, and he grunted from the force of impact. Already the brave lad had another projectile in flight. Lew dodged it and threw a shot in the youngster's direction. It caused the boy to dive away from the threat.

"Head 'em up! Head 'em up!" Lew shouted, although his men had only gathered some thirty-five or so Appaloosies. "Let's get outta here."

Sounds of gunfire carried clearly to the five clan villages of *Peopeo Kiskiak Hihi's* band. Often, since the first whites had invaded their peaceful country, they had heard similar disturbances. The men tensed and the women wore anxious expressions. What could it mean?

Soon the firing stopped. Many among the lodges sought to ignore it. Who could account for the vagueries of the whites? Not so, a visiting young warrior named *Wahlitits*.

"Soon they'll come and murder us in our sleep,"

15

Wahlitits grumbled to six of his friends. "This land is free. It belongs to no one. Yet they say it is now theirs. The animals on it are for all, the whites say no, only for them. I know what this sound means. They're stealing your horses. Come. We'll go and fight them."

Several men shouted agreement. Others looked worried, including several of the council. Pounding hoofbeats could be heard hurrying toward the villages. *Wahlitits* pointed in that direction.

"Hear? They come now to destroy us. We must fight!"

"No," the camp herald shouted over a babble of excited voices. "They are Silver Eel and Spotted Salmon. Our herd boys are returning."

The rapid approach of the sweaty youths soon proved the keenness of the camp crier's eyes. They galloped in on foam-flecked horses and slid to the ground, tossing their braided horsehair guide ropes to other children who had rushed forward.

"White men. They killed Hawk and Blue Buffalo, *Wayowits* and Beaver Lodge. They steal our horses," Silver Eel shouted shrilly.

"How many?" *Wahlitits* demanded.

"Three hands of men. One did not get away. Hawk shot him with an arrow and he fell under the hoofs of our ponies," Spotted Salmon panted out.

"We'll go after them," the fiery young warrior shouted.

"We should take this to the white man's army, *Wahlitits*," an elder counseled.

"To the dark pit with the army! They kill your boy children and steal your horses. We will avenge this ourselves," *Wahlitits* cried passionately. "Who goes with me?"

16

"I do!"

"And I."

"We're with you, *Wahlitits*."

Before the special war horses had been gathered, the men painted and made ready, a full twenty young warriors of the five clans banding behind *Wahlitits* to get revenge on the evil whites. Wide-eyed, Silver Eel and Spotted Salmon stood watching as the braves put daubs of paint on the faces, necks, and chests of their mounts.

"I wish I were going along," Spotted Salmon declared fervently.

"So do I. Only . . . Spotted Salmon, what if we were killed?"

"Don't be a foolish girl-child, Silver Eel. There is nothing more glorious for a man than to die in battle as a warrior."

"Sometimes . . . I'm not so sure of that," the smaller boy answered uncertainly.

Following the white men had been childishly simple. Thirty-plus spotted horses left a wide, clear trail. *Wahlitits* and his war party raced over the ground. Ahead, a haze of dust near the big bend of the Salmon River betrayed the position of their enemy. Headlong the warriors dashed across an open camas meadow to be met with a wall of puffy gunsmoke.

Bullets whined and moaned through the air and a Nez Percé brave cried out as he flung his arms wide and flipped from the saddle. Another line of powder smoke spewed from the trees. A churning spotted stallion whinnied shrilly and crashed chest first to the ground. Its rider vaulted over its dying head and tucked his body into

17

a roll.

"Divide!" *Wahlitits* shouted.

The Nez Percé split to right and left. Several men fired arrows at the invisible enemy, then streaked off.

"To me! To me!" *Wahlitits* commanded and the men quickly reformed.

Another charge met with even less success.

Two beautiful horses died and another brave had his spine shattered by a heavy .44-40 slug. He died screaming in agony. Mocking laughter sounded from among the trees as the enemy withdrew.

Determined, *Wahlitits* pressed after the fleeing whites. The strong, intelligent spotted horses threaded through the stands of alder, spruce, and fir, pushing after the flitting shapes of their masters' hated foes. Now and then a shot sounded. Bark sprayed or a twig flew away. It seemed only moments before the steady rush of the Salmon could be heard once more. The ford.

Wahlitits thought of it with renewed bitterness. He and his warriors could be easily slaughtered crossing there. To go along the bank to another easy passage would be to lose the enemy altogether. He urged his followers on.

"We will catch them in the water. Hurry."

They didn't. And the bristle of rifle barrels on the far shore discouraged any further pursuit. Two men and three precious spotted-rump horses had been lost, not counting the thirty-seven stolen by the whites. Some day they would have to be punished for this.

Some day, *Wahlitits* vowed as he shook an impotent fist at the retreating white men, he would exact full payment for the horses, men, and boys murdered this bright morning.

Chapter 2

Birds twittered in the cottonwood and jack pine. A warm, yellow globe hung in the cerulean sky. Its heat had eliminated the night's frost within half an hour after sunrise. To one of the two persons squatting beside a campfire, omens presaged a glorious day.

"I *know* it's October, Lone Wolf," the attractive young woman said as she gave an angry toss to the ebony braids that lay on her slim shoulders. Her small, graceful hands cradled a tin cup of steaming Arbuckle's coffee. "And I *know* it's a long way we have to ride. Even so, I want to go on to Oregon and buy or trade for a Palousie horse. Since I lost Boots in that train wreck in Missouri, I haven't been satisfied with any replacement we've been able to get. Boots was a fine Morgan. These spotted-rump horses of the Nez Percé are considered to be even better."

"All, of course, to your credit as a judge of fine horse flesh, Rebecca," her lanky, blond-haired companion answered dryly. "Only we have all of Idaho to cross, the first snows have long since fallen in the high passes, and we have no guide."

"We have ourselves," Rebecca Caldwell snapped. Her blue eyes blazed with inner fire, a sure sign Lone

Wolf had seen many times. "The Nez Percé are in Idaho as well. Once we've made a deal, we should still have time to cross the Cascades and then turn south to California. Or go south in the desert and take the Mormon Road through the coastal mountains to San Diego. I've heard there are places there where it never snows."

Brett Baylor, who after ten years of semi-captivity with the Crow preferred to call himself Lone Wolf, snorted derisively. "The hucksters have been peddling California to the gullible since the gold rush. Outside of a desert or the swamps in Florida, show me a place where it doesn't snow."

"I still want to go," Rebecca said primly. She smoothed a wrinkle in her white elkhide dress in seeming indifference.

That ended the discussion.

Lone Wolf tossed thick slices off the bacon slab into a smoking cast-iron skillet. Strong, square-jawed face still averted from his partner, he added some slices of raw potato and a chopped chili pepper. Then he looked askance at her over one Crow-hunting, shirt-clad shoulder.

A rueful smile flickered a moment before he shaped it into one of cheery agreement.

"Fort Missoula is only a day's ride ahead. If we push it, we can be through the Bitterroot Mountains and halfway across the panhandle of Idaho in eight more days. I suppose, with luck, we can avoid what happened to the Donner party."

"Oh, Lone Wolf, don't be such an old settin' hen."

"We'll go to California, Becky, because you want to," he relented.

Impulsively, Rebecca reached out and hugged him,

20

then planted a chaste kiss on his forehead. Despite his years of hardship and bloodshed, Lone Wolf managed a blush.

A satellite community had grown up around Fort Missoula. The army post, actually too small to be called a fort, maintained a garrison of some three hundred men. The usual services desired by soldiers had come first: saloons, bawdy houses, a barbershop, and a bathhouse. Then "civilizing" forces had moved in. Two mercantiles competed for trade, while a small hotel nestled between a feuding pair of restaurants, each engaged in a price war with the other.

"Full course meal: 50 cts." had been crossed out on one sign, and "35 cts." written below it. On the other dining emporium, the sandwich board sign at the edge of the boardwalk proclaiming "Full course meal: 40 cts." had been struck through and replaced with "25 cts." At the first establishment, a man in a white apron, black trousers, and a white shirt bent over and drew a line through the thirty-five cents. He began to write ten cents as Rebecca and Lone Wolf rode into town.

"One of them is going out of business before long," Rebecca observed.

"Any bets on which one?" Lone Wolf replied, pointing to where another harassed-looking man hurried from the second cafe and began to alter his sign.

"No. That fellah has the right idea," Rebecca declared.

Under the slashed-off twenty-five cents advertisement, the proprietor hastily lettered in: "Two for the price of one."

Lone Wolf chuckled. They turned in at the tie-rail in front of the hotel and dismounted. A sign near the front door of the hostelry advertised its own livery for guests. Inside, the pair stopped before the registration counter, little more than a pulpitlike pedestal with a hinged, slanted desk surface and a registry book on a swivel mount.

"Yess, folks," an aging man in sleeve protectors and a green eyeshade hissed at them.

"We need two rooms. At the back if possible, second floor," Lone Wolf recited as though from memory.

"I can put the lady up that way if you like. Only other back room I've got is on the ground floor."

"That'll be fine," Rebecca injected.

"Sign here please." The clerk spun the register in their direction and turned away to reach for keys hung from cup hooks on a polished wooden plaque tacked to the wall. "Here ya are, Room Twenty-three and Eleven. One night iss it?"

"Yes," Lone Wolf informed him.

"You have horssesss to board?"

"Of course."

"That'll be two dollarss, cash in advance."

Lone Wolf reached into the watch pocket of his trousers and fished out a three-dollar gold piece. He and Rebecca had stopped a mile from town and changed into "white man's clothing," in order not to attract undue attention.

The desk man produced a silver dollar in return and slapped a bell push with a dry, age-chafed palm. "Front, boy."

For a moment, Rebecca thought her heart would stop. Bobby here?

22

Approaching them came a small lad, with the same shock of curly blond hair, soft brown eyes, and frosting of freckles that Bobby Rhodes possessed; familiar features that had become so precious to Rebecca Caldwell. A tiny gasp escaped her and she placed a hand over her heart. But Bobby was in Kansas. With a visible effort, Rebecca shook off the enchantment this youngster had inspired and smiled weakly.

"Yes, sir," the boy rushed out in a voice not yet settled into its change.

The clerk looked inquisitively at Lone Wolf. "Saddle bags on the two mounts outside and the parfleches on the packhorse."

"Room Eleven for the man, Twenty-three for the lady. Then put their horses up in the stable," the reptilian voice of the clerk added.

"Right away." Quickly the youngster headed for the double front doors.

Rebecca and Lone Wolf turned and walked away from the desk. "Didn't he look like . . ." they both began. Then laughter bubbled up.

"Yes, he did," Rebecca said firmly. "Almost exactly like Bobby Rhodes."

"Uh . . . are you getting any, ah, ideas?"

"N-no. No, of course not," Rebecca answered a bit too quickly.

"Shame on you. Corrupting children," Lone Wolf chided, not entirely frivolously.

"You're right. He *is* a child. Bobby was nearly seventeen."

"Be a good girl, then, and I'll see you at supper time."

*   *   *

"Here you are, Ma'am. Your bags," the bright-eyed youth announced.

It had happened again when Rebecca opened the door. She could hardly believe the resemblance. For a long moment she stood unmoving, staring. She realized her mouth hung slightly open and she moved to cover her embarrassing lapse.

"Uh, oh, yes. Come on in." The boy entered and Rebecca closed the door behind him. "Forgive me for staring like that. It happens I have a, ah, good friend in Kansas who looks almost exactly like you. His name is Bobby Rhodes."

"Two boys so far apart who look alike? That's p'culiar, isn't it. Where would you like these?"

"Over there will be fine. Put the saddlebags on the, ah, bed."

The boy did as bidden and turned to Rebecca with a sweet smile, expecting a tip. Rebecca stepped closer, one hand in her reticule, searching for a coin.

"What is your name?" she inquired as she handed him a quarter. When the lad reached out for it, she noticed that, like Bobby, he bit his nails.

"Sammy, Ma'am. Sammy Graham. And, ah, thank you. That's the most generous tip I've ever gotten."

"You deserve it." Rebecca still did not step out of his pathway to the door. "Bobby's eighteen now, going on nineteen."

Sammy blushed slightly. "I'm seventeen. But everyone says I'm too small for my age."

"Why, so is Bobby."

A powerful stirring deep within her loins pained Rebecca, and she felt her heartbeat increase with the awakening of long unsatisfied desire. She wet suddenly

24

dry lips with a pink snippet of tongue and let her gaze declaim her need as she took in Sammy's small stature and delightfully angelic features.

"I really am seventeen, though, Ma'am."

"I'm Rebecca, Sammy. Have you any other duties? Or . . . can you stay a while?"

She inclined her small, well-shaped breasts toward the boy and smiled an invitation that only the densest of males could misinterpret. Sammy flushed to the roots of his yellow hair, the color seeping past the tight collar of his shirt. He fidgeted like a much younger child, hands behind his back, and part of the reason for his nervousness advertised itself by a rising protrusion in his trousers.

"I, ah, gee, I guess I can stay a little while, Miss Rebecca. If . . . if you want me to."

A light trill of laughter bubbled up and tickled Rebecca's lips. "Want you? Oh, Sammy, you have no idea how much I, ah, want you."

No dullard, Sammy took on a deeper crimson hue as the meaning of her words became clear. This wasn't the first time he had received less than thinly veiled offers of a similar nature. He twisted at the waist more rapidly and looked down to study the toes of his shoes.

"I, uh, ain't too knowin' about those sorts of things, Rebecca," Sammy said quietly, his innate shyness and present embarrassment confounding him.

His rebellious body raged with wild longings that his conscience struggled to deny. Worse, he had developed a throbbing, unbelievably sensitive erection that just had to be shoving out the front of his trousers like a flagpole in a tent. Sammy's heart pounded against his thin chest so that he swore she could hear it. And he discovered that

25

his mouth and throat had gone dry.

Rebecca stepped closer, putting a small, soft hand on his chest. Beneath the cloth and flesh she felt his heart racing and smiled a secret smile.

"Neither had Bobby . . . till he met me. I, ah, would be happy to, er, help you, uh, teach you a little. If, that is, you really wanted to?"

Sammy swallowed with difficulty. He'd often dreamed of this sort of thing when he lay in his solitary bed, choking his chicken—as the boys around town called self-pleasure. Working in a hotel naturally invited such fantasies. But he'd never come so close to realizing his imagined happiness.

"Uh . . . I, ah, YES!" Shocked at the urgency of his words, Sammy cleared his throat and tried to sound manly and sophisticated. "Er, that is, uh, sure, I suppose so. I, uh-uh, I'd like that, yeah." His pose dissolved into a turmoil of insecurity and confusion. "I mean, if you . . . uh, you really wanted to fool around with someone dumb as me."

Rebecca leaned down and brushed her lips lightly across Sammy's. "You're not dumb, Sammy. Only uneducated. And I, oh-so-much, want to be your teacher."

She whirled away and sat lightly on the side of the bed. A coy expression fixed on Rebecca's face as she patted the cover beside her.

"Come over here, Sammy, and sit beside me."

Eyes wide, glowing with the intensity of his virginal passion, Sammy walked stiff-legged to the bed. He sat woodenly beside Rebecca waiting for the harsh words or cruel laughter that would burst his hopes apart. Instead, he felt fingers fumbling in his lap, then coolness as

Rebecca slid her hand behind his waistband and plunged downward.

"First off, let's see what we have here," she said with an almost brittle brightness.

Her eyes widened as her facile digits encircled the surprisingly thick base of Sammy's heated phallus. Her pulse burned as she slid her hand upward, taking mental inventory of his endowments. She enjoyed the feel of his pleasing length of warm, satiny flesh, rigid and slightly tapered. Sammy groaned as she gently slid her hand over his rock-hard length. Back and forth . . . back and forth.

Never gaining speed, the slow, delicious rhythm continued as Sammy's hands flew to the front of his trousers, his fingers fumbling to undo the buttons of his fly. Frantically he yanked down the top of his summer-weight long johns.

A delightful tingling sensation rippled outward from Sammy's groin as the cool air in the room caressed his throbbing maleness. Rebecca's eyes widened with happy anticipation when she observed his generous propor-tions. Far from the largest she had known, it yet held the promise of a night of infinite delights. Rebecca stopped stroking him and spanned his reddened organ with her thumb and little finger.

"I, uh, it's, ummm, five and a half, ah, inches," Sammy stammered through his embarrassment. For a fleeting moment his stern upbringing reasserted itself. "Ah, ummm, Miss Rebecca, er, it's, ah, it's awful hard to be good right now," he pleaded.

Abruptly she stopped manipulating him and gave the boy an odd, hungry look. "Sammy, believe me, it's *got* to be hard to be good. Now lay back on the bed for a little while, hummm?"

With a sigh of willing resignation, Sammy complied. Rebecca slid from her perch beside him and knelt between his legs. Her blue eyes twinkled with delight and she bent forward expectantly. Once again she began to stroke his hard burning flesh. Slowly she lowered her lips over his stiffened member. A cascade of her raven hair spilled onto the pale skin of his lower belly.

Sammy shivered with ecstacy, then trembled again as her tongue worked its blissful magic. He gasped in outrageous euphoria and raised upward from the bed, poised on his shoulders and feet. Though the boy had no way of knowing it, she took as incredible a pleasure in the act as he did. Her own powerful cravings had become almost unbearable and she hurried to bring him to completion so they could move on to new adventures.

When it came, however, it seemed entirely too soon to Rebecca. She stood before his limp body and beckoned invitingly.

"Sit up and I'll undress you, then you can do the same for me."

Weakened by his frantic sexual release, Sammy gulped and pushed himself upright. The light of ardor had not left his eyes.

"N-now what?" he stammered.

"Now you advance to the second grade." Rebecca reached out and pulled Sammy's shirt over his head. "Be quick. Undo the fasteners of my dress and help me out of it."

Inexpertly, Sammy complied. He felt his fervor once again rising as her creamy, lightly bronzed flesh became exposed to his avid examination. She trembled slightly, in heated anxiety, as he slid the clothing away. He nearly choked over his excitement at the sight of her small, dark-tipped breasts and flat, firm belly, rounded invitingly.

Excitedly she squeezed one breast. "Oh, hurry, take it in your mouth," Rebecca panted. "Please, Sammy."

Sammy opened wide and bent close, his warm breath thrilling her as he closed sweet, eager lips over her hardened nipple. Rebecca quivered all over.

"Aaah! Ayeeee! Yes, that's it. More . . . harder . . . yes—yes—yes."

Quivering constantly now, she reached out and gently disengaged him. A fine sheen of passionate moisture glossed her skin as she lay on the bed and spread her legs invitingly. Struck dumb on the moment of his departure from childhood, Sammy could only gape at her treasures.

"Come to me, Sammy, make me happy."

Awkwardly, Sammy climbed onto the bed. How beautiful the arched flare of her rib cage, he thought. A heady scent filled his nostrils and he was overcome by a strong, powerful urge.

Shaking like fall's last leaf, Sammy descended on her velvet flesh. Rebecca writhed and squealed while he gave them both unbounded joy. She reached out and encased his rock-hard shaft in one moist hand, squeezing and stroking with a frantic rhythm. Time stood still as the magnificent engagement went on until they both reached the ultimate peak of pleasure.

This would be one long, wonderful night, Rebecca thought, as she stretched seductively on the tousled bed. Her amorous nature clamored for her to find again with Sammy that special sort of fulfillment she'd first discovered with Bobby Rhodes.

She'd miss her supper engagement with Lone Wolf, Rebecca realized.

But, who cared? Who cared?

Chapter 3

Young lips, eager lips, nuzzling and nibbling at her breast. Could it be possible? A fifth time? Yes, oh, yes. Her breath quickened as she felt Sammy's hardness pressing into her side. She reached for him and guided her seventeen-year-old lover atop her fevered body. Slowly he entered her . . .

Rebecca Caldwell roughly shoved the vivid, too-stimulating images away and drew a shaky breath. The insistent massaging of her loins was being done by her saddle, not the shy-but-anxious youngster she had so joyfully initiated into the mysteries of love the night before. Slowly the heat of remembered passion subsided and she cleared her throat.

"Isn't this beautiful country out here?" she called over the steady clop of their horses walking.

"It's that, all right," Lone Wolf agreed. "Almost makes it worth the trip."

"You're teasing again," Rebecca accused.

Lone Wolf gave her an easy smile. "Of course. You know, now that we've started, I'm glad we're going."

They had left before sunup. Drained, and feeling oh-so-thoroughly loved, Rebecca had ample stamina for their journey. Some twenty miles separated them from Fort Missoula, and the sharp angle of the sun at their backs made it only mid-morning. At this rate they would be well into Idaho by nightfall. That thought greatly pleased the raven-haired half-Sioux beauty.

"I can't wait to see herds of those marvelous spotted-rump ponies," Rebecca enthused. "I remember the first time I saw one. Only one. A horse trader rode him. He came to Iron Claw's village. I was sixteen at the time and had just fallen madly in love with Four Horns. . . ."

. . . Children scurried around, squealing with excitment as the *eyanpaha* made his rounds of the camp crying the arrival of a horse trader. Bright expectation glowed in the eyes of the young men, and their elders licked lips in anticipation of the pleasure to be had in the bargaining. Rebecca Caldwell stood with a small group of marriageable-aged girls near the big lodge of the chief, Iron Claw. The youthful Oglala girls tittered and made salacious comments about the distended organs on several of the stallions driven past them by the trader.

"Oh, look," Red Shawl exclaimed. "That one makes me think of Walking Elk."

"Walking Elk?" one of her companions declared scornfully. "We cooked a puppy for supper last night who was better gifted than Walking Elk. Now if you ask me, which none of you did, I'd say that painted stallion is more like Four Horns."

Caught off guard, Rebecca blurted out, "Why, that's what I was thinking."

She flushed and that brought on another gush of giggles. Red Shawl pinched her on the arm. "Oh? *How* would you know, *Sinaskawin?*"

"I . . . er, never mind." Rebecca blushed deeper red.

31

Peals of giggles.

"Wh-a-at kind of horse is that?" Chokecherry Bird gulped in an awed voice.

"He's beautiful!" Red Shawl agreed.

"Oh, oh, I've never seen such a pretty horse before," Sunflower gasped dramatically.

"There'll be no trading for him," Rebecca said wisely. "See, he's being ridden by the trader. Whatever it is, wherever he got it, he'd give up his scalp lock before he'd dispose of that one."

Like everyone in the village, Rebecca found she could hardly take her eyes off the coal-black and cloud-white coat of the gorgeous creature. The ebony spots that freckled its alabaster rump and loins fascinated her. Gradually she began to make out other characteristics that only added to its beauty.

The proudly aloof stallion had parti-colored skin about its nostrils and lips and around its genitals. It had an unusually short mane and tail, not roached and trimmed, but grown that way. There were white sclera in its eyes and it had prominent, well-defined withers, which gave it a sturdier look than other horses. Her heart quickened and she knew the first fire of an unquenchable yearning. . . .

". . . I've never stopped wanting one," Rebecca confided to Lone Wolf. "After that time I didn't see another, until a friendly party of Cheyenne came to visit the same year I met you and escaped from the Oglala. Four of their warriors had Palousie horses. It was from them I learned where the breed originated."

"And now your wish is going to come true, eh?"

"I certainly hope so."

*   *   *

32

Whickering nervously to each other, thirty-seven spotted-rump horses trotted along the main street of the fledgling hamlet of Pendleton, Oregon. At the head of the string of stolen horses rode Lew Gorce, along with Sy Burton and a ferret-faced individual named Red Ashton. More of the rustler gang rode the flanks, while Clem Dye and Niel Thorne ate dust on the drag. As they passed the Timbers Saloon, an old-timer began to slap his hat on his thigh and dance a little jig.

"Hey, fellers!" he shouted to the men inside. "Lookie here. A whole passel of Appaloosie horses. Man-oh-man, what a sight."

"The boss ain't gonna have any trouble sellin' these," Sy Burton observed as a crowd of men flocked out of the saloon onto the boardwalk.

"Yeah," Red Ashton grumbled. "We do the work an' he makes the profit."

"You get your share, same as everybody else," Lew snapped. "Hold yer tongue, Red, or you might hafta eat some knuckles."

"You callin' me?" The auburn-haired gunhawk snarled, instantly on the prod.

"I was thinkin' of Mr. Styles. But . . . if he don't want the pleasure, I'd sure be obliged. Don't get so proddy, ya little weasel. I'm near a foot taller and sixty pounds heavier. Best be holdin' yer temper or light a shuck outta here." Lew nodded, a pointing gesture that directed attention toward a man standing in the street, three blocks ahead.

"There's Mr. Styles now. Remember, Red, we're all in this for the money. You'll get yours."

"You damn betcha I will," the surly half-pint growled.

Lew raised in the saddle and waved his hat in a circle over his head. "Let's bring 'em in in style, boys!"

Whoops and hollers from the drovers jumped the thirty-seven Palouses into a brisk trot that quickly became a dust-raising gallop. Far ahead, Roger Styles ran to a pole corral and swung open a large gate that nearly blocked off the entire width of the street. Lew and his two henchmen aimed their mounts for the open end, where their boss waited. They arrived in a shower of dirt and dried horse droppings that enveloped the tall, potbellied man standing in the gap.

"Here they are, Mr. Styles," Lew cried. "Thirty-seven of the finest Appaloosies you'll ever see."

"Good work, Lew. You and the boys can all take a draw of a hundred each to lubricate yourselves. There's more of 'em out there and we'll want you to be on the move soon."

Roger Styles's long, spatulate fingers brushed lightly at the smattering of white hairs at his left temple. Matched on the right by another spray, these and the wrinkles of worry and dissipation around his eyes and mouth normally indicated a man considerably older than Roger. He had suffered aplenty and endured a lot, frequently being forced to face disaster and adversity beyond his thirty-odd years. Given to a flamboyant style and rich living, it showed in his mound of stomach and the fine tailoring of his expensive suit.

"Sure thing, Boss," Lew acknowledged. "We lost one man. Little bit of a Nez Percé kid shot him in the leg and he fell under the horses' hoofs."

"Too bad. We'll divide his share among the rest of you. Who was it, by the way?"

"Beauregarde Bettles."

"Humm. Small loss. He was a braggart. The rest of you are here safe and alive and bent on some serious drinking, no doubt?"

"You bet, Boss. We have a couple of days, at least, don't we?"

"Oh, of course. Then, back after those Nez Percé horses. Get them put away and come over to the office. I'll give you the advance pay for the boys."

"Thank you, Mr. Styles."

After the horses had been corralled and Lew Gorce had left the office with a small leather bag of twenty-dollar gold pieces, Roger Styles poured three glasses of fine brandy. One for himself, the others for the two men seated in comfortable chairs close by his rolltop desk.

"Here's to success, gentlemen," Roger toasted.

"Here, here," Clive Reversford drawled in his lazy, upper-class English accent. He had folded his tall, lean body into the leather cushions and his long horsey face beamed with anticipation.

"Cheers to all of us," Jason Brill declared, hoisting his glass.

Cold blue eyes fixed on the banker, while Clive sent his question to Roger. "I say, Roger old boy, how much do you anticipate making on these brutes?"

Roger kept his gaze on the careless arrangement of yellow locks that crowned Reversford's lobey head. "More than enough to cover those advances, if that's what's worrying you, Clive."

"Ra-ther, I should hope. Fifteen hundred dollars, labeled as an 'advance,' is one hell of a lot of money. I should think horseflesh wouldn't bring more than thirty-five, forty dollars a head around here."

"It won't. We've been over it all before, Clive."

"Humor me and tell it again."

"Really," the squeaky-voiced banker, Brill, inserted. "Isn't this all a waste of time?"

"Not at all, old pip," Clive barked flippantly. "I really

35

do want to be assured. Terribly insecure, don't chew know?"

"Very good," Roger interrupted to get the conversation on course and finished. "We sell the first ones here, at whatever rate the traffic will bear. That way it sort of makes everyone around who owns one a part of the whole deal. They'll sure never back any Nez Percé's complaint that the critters were stolen. These are not ordinary horses, as you saw. So we aren't asking ordinary prices. Say we start at seventy-five dollars. That makes . . ."

"Ummmm, two thousand seven hundred seventy-five dollars," Jason Brill's banker mind immediately supplied. "But surely we're going to keep back sufficient quantity of stallions to provide for ourselves, aren't we?" His deep-set eyes, oddly defying a classification of color, flashed yellow with greed.

A sheen of perspiration glowed on the large bald spot in the middle of his shaggy tonsure of graying hair. Brill patted his protruding belly and adjusted the knife-crease of his suit trousers. A small, pursed bow mouth would have given him an effeminate appearance, except for the porcine jowls and strange, receded eyes.

"At a minimum, that would be three horses. Four, if you count our, ah, silent partner. Removing them from the market would eat up profits of . . ."

"Only three hundred dollars," Brill snapped out. "To say the least, I think we deserve them before anyone else."

"That still doesn't explain how our profits keep ahead of what we're paying the men who bring the animals here." Reversford injected.

"I'm glad you reminded me of that," Roger said, meaning it. "To get back to the subject at question, Clive,

36

Jason, we continue to put out these little, ah, advances when each herd come in. Enough of them, large enough, so that when it comes time to settle up and pay Gorce and his men on the valuable animals we sell back east or in Europe, they'll simply have 'used up' all their shares. Though we won't have paid them nearly half of what they actually have coming. And we'll be the richer by over thirty thousand dollars." Roger reached into a pigeon-hole of his desk and produced a sheaf of letters.

"The orders have been coming in, gentlemen. I've neglected to mention that, but all the same, here they are." Glancing down, Roger began to read off figures.

"A thousand dollars for a stud. Eight hundred for a mare in foal. Seventeen hundred for a pair to be shipped to Paris. A matador—whatever the hell that is—in Lisbon wants four yearlings, and will pay twelve hundred each. And two or more of those can be geldings. The money's out there, gentlemen. All we have to do is reach out and grab it."

"You paint a most rosy picture, Roger," Clive drawled. "One I'm most tempted to accept. In fact, I do. Now what's on the agenda for the future?"

"We'll be sending Lew and the boys out day after tomorrow. I've heard from my sources of two fairly large herds close to each other. We want a clean sweep. And to see to it, I think I'll be going along."

"Good Lord! Are you serious? Roger Styles roughing it?"

"I'd like you to come along, too, Clive."

"'Pon my word. Into the . . . the wilderness?"

"Sure." Roger grinned wickedly. "It'll do you good. You're putting on a bit of a pot, don't chew know?" he mocked the Englishman in an affected accent.

Chapter 4

Winding sinuously from southeast to northwest across Idaho, the Snake River rushed mightily along its banks. Fed by mountain freshets and falls, the cold water had an aura of urgency about it. To Rebecca Caldwell, crossing it seemed a lovely, inviting adventure.

She and Lone Wolf stood talking terms with a trio of ill-kempt, scruffy examples of the worst in human kind. Untrimmed and unwashed, their odorous bodies exuding an almost tangible effluvium of foulness, the three river rats flashed yellowed, broken teeth and scratched some part of their soiled bodies constantly.

"We-ll now, the river's way up, 'count of the rains," the eldest of the obnoxious trio whined for the fourth time. "Ain't rightly safe to make a crossin'. What you think, Brother Jethro?"

"Oh, that's the plain truth of it, it is. Ain't that so, Cousin Jaspar?"

"Shore's I's born, it is. Jist like Cousin Jo-Ray said. Only a fool'd go out on that water now. 'Least not for less 'n, ah, say five dollars, gold."

"Per person," Jethro added.

"Same fer each animal," Jo-Ray contributed.

"Where's your masks and guns?" Lone Wolf growled.

"Say what?" Jaspar queried, blank-faced, blinking flat, gray eyes.

"Most road agents wear a bandanna to cover their faces," the white warrior patiently explained his quip. "And somehow, I get the feeling you're trying to hold us up."

"Now, that's no way to talk to decent fo'ks, is it, Mister?" Jo-Ray whined.

"Decent is as decent does," Rebecca added sweetly.

Her lovely blue eyes had turned icy, a warning the unpleasant trio had never experienced before. Unfortunately, they ignored what they didn't recognize. Jaspar gave her a withering stare.

"Missy, yer a right purty li'l thing. But this here is man talk, and I'd be 'bliged if you kept outta it."

Fine Green River steel edged Rebecca's words. "And I'd be obliged if you stopped trying to gouge us until we bled. Five dollars for the lot of us. Be damned glad you're getting that. We could simply take this ferry of yours at gunpoint."

Tobacco juice stained the graying stubble on Jo-Ray's hollow cheeks. He rolled his eyes in a peculiar fashion, showing lots of white, and spat at the forehoofs of Rebecca's horse.

"An' what if we was to up an' cut that-there towrope?"

"Dead men do little cutting," Rebecca informed them coldly.

The three scroungers eyed the brace of saddle holsters on Rebecca's pommel. Polished walnut grips advertised the presence of her pair of Smith and Wesson Americans. Jo-Ray worried his cud of plug around from one side of his mouth to the other. Jethro licked his thin, bloodless lips. Jaspar reached down and groped his crotch, in search of some breed of pesky vermin.

"Five dollars, the lady said. That's our last offer before we simply make the crossing without you," Lone Wolf told them lightly, enjoying it.

"Five . . . dollars . . . includin' the packhorse?"

"Five dollars, Jo-Ray," Rebecca responded flatly.

"Why, jingoes, that ain't hardly enough to keep body an' soul together . . . I think . . ."

"Shut up, Jo-Ray," Rebecca commanded sharply. "You don't think. That's your problem. You've heard our offer. Take it or leave it."

Again they eyed the ready six-guns.

"Done. An' cheap at half the price," Jo-Ray surrendered.

Unrelenting, Rebecca pointed to a crudely lettered sign tacked to the side of the odorous shack that served as home and office for the ferrymen. "Then what's that sign say about 'two bits per person, fifteen cents per animal?'"

"'Taint fair. That's for when the river's way down," Jethro complained.

"Then pretend it's down now. It's that . . ." Rebecca reached out to pat the butt of one Smith American. "Or do it the hard way."

Lew Gorce studied Roger Styles through the haze of dust that rose from the dry ground they covered at a walk. For all his dandified clothes—today, English riding pants and high, leg-hugging boots—and his liking for expensive liquor and refined dining, the boss rode a horse like a natural and took the hardships of the trail without complaining. He'd do, Lew decided.

Somewhere in his past, Styles had to have encountered rough living aplenty. It showed in a man: the way he carried himself, made do around camp, such like. Not at all like that sissy, Reversford, who had turned back the second day on the trail. Lew smiled thinking of it. No, Styles had grit.

Tough, for sure, for all his soft face and hands. Styles could shoot, too. Yesterday he'd downed a deer for supper with a snap shot from horseback. When they got to the Indians, that's where he'd see what Styles was really made of. They might be savages, but *they* fought back. Lew caught sight of movement ahead and cut off his evaluation with a grunt.

"Somethin' up there, Mister Styles."

"I saw it. An animal of some sort. What else could it be?"

Lew peered intently at the blaze of gold and scarlet alder leaves. "The Nez Percés, out lookin' for us."

"Shit. What we don't need now is a gun battle. Everyone for miles around would know we're here."

"What do you figger we should do?" Lew inquired with genuine concern.

"We don't make a run for it, that's for certain sure. What say you and I go have a look at our mysterious beast?"

Gorce's face brightened with a pleased grin. "I like your style, uh, Boss."

"Make that Roger, Lew. Time's a wastin'."

They rode forward at a brisk trot. Halfway to where they had sighted the unknown creature, they split apart without the need to discuss it, then disappeared off the thread of trail they followed into the thick stands of alder, birch, and pine. Five minutes of nothing but the sound of thrashing horses' hoofs followed. Then Roger Styles's voice sounded, strong, but tinted with awe.

"Oh . . . shit. I just cornered a bear."

A hollow, vengeful roar verified his startled announcement.

"Be right there, Roger," Lew Gorce sang out.

How were they going to handle this? Lew pondered it as he urged his mount through the thick brush and clinging limbs. Too close to the Nez Percé to shoot the bear. Maybe, just maybe, Roger could back off before the bear decided to attack. No. The minute they turned their backs, the brute would rush them. What could they do? A moment later, he saw Roger's broad back.

Beyond Roger, a huge furry shape swayed upright on hind legs, front paws swiping at the air like a pugilist. Blatantly male, the seven foot grizzly threw back its head and bellowed again. Roger's horse screamed shrilly and reared, nearly unseating its rider.

Quick thinking saved Styles from serious injury as he kicked free of the stirrups and slid off before the frightened animal went over backward and fell heavily on its left side. Roger's hand came away from his saddle skirt clutching the heavy hilt of the longest knife Lew had ever seen. More a sword than a dagger. Roger, too, knew better than to use a firearm. The bear uttered a snuffling grunt and waddled forward.

Swift as spring lightning, the grizzly made a blurred swipe and disemboweled the shrieking horse. Roger danced back out of the animal's reach and darted the fine tip of his weapon forward and back with the skill and speed of a weaver's shuttle. Tiny flecks of red began to appear on the bear's coat. Lew Gorce edged his mount to

42

the side and unloosed a tomahawk from where he secured it by a latigo tie. He hefted the weapon and watched while the grizzly lumbered to its left and sent Roger sprawling with a backhand cuff.

Roger hit the ground rolling and came up, short sword point upward and ready. Speedily for an animal of such great size, the bear moved in, swaying, swatting his paws. Like liquid light, Roger wove a pattern with his blade. Blood began to drip from the beast's forelegs.

"Keep him busy, Roger. I'll work around behind, come at his spine with this."

Styles didn't even look, only nodded, full, sensuous lips pulled into a menacing snarl. "Do it quick. I can't hold out too much longer."

Another mighty bellow came from the shaggy bruin and it leaped at Roger, brushing aside the frail defense of the sword. It wrapped powerful forelegs around Roger's chest and began to rake its long, ugly claws at his back, while it squeezed with bone-crushing pressure. Working in close, Roger started to stab deeply into the side of the bear's abdomen.

Face twisted in agony, Roger continued to plunge his oddly shaped weapon into the fat-padded side of the foul-breathed creature. He worked upward, sliding the blade between ribs, searching for lung or heart. Lew side-stepped his horse around into position. Then he urged his frightened mount forward and swung with all his might.

The tomahawk made a solid, smacking sound as it bit into the muscles of the bear's back. Keen steel sliced through to the bone, before it halted abruptly. Lew felt the shock all the way to his shoulder. With a powerful wrench, he freed the 'hawk and struck again before the bear could turn to confront this new tormentor.

43

"Now!" Lew shouted. "Stick him good."

Roger needed no prompting. The grizzly turned on Lew and Roger lined up on the position of the right kidney. He drove his short sword to the hilt. Then again . . . and a third time. Despite the pain in his chest and the blood-spilling cuts on his back, he jumped nimbly to the left and buried his blade in the opposite side of the huge animal's back.

An almost feminine scream came from the grizzly. It shuddered, stiffened upright, and then toppled onto one side. Its legs thrashed helplessly as the dying spasms quaked through its body. Standing over its carcass, Roger swayed and sank to his knees.

"Jesus Christ!"

"Wrestlin' a bear's hardly my idea of an afternoon's entertainment, Roger," Lew panted out.

"Nor mine. What do we do with him?"

"Bear's greasy meat."

"He smells of fish, too," Roger added, thinking of the unsavory breath the grizzly puffed into his face.

"Probably taste awful."

"Let's leave him."

"Fine with me, Roger. Say, what the hell kind of a blade is that thing you were usin'?"

Still panting, Styles hefted the heavy length of steel. "It's a throwback, really. A Model 'Forty-nine Ames Rifleman's knife. Wicked bastard, once you learn how to handle it right."

Gorce shook his head in admiration. "You sure did that, all right."

Neither man spoke for a while. Roger cleaned his Ames and stripped the saddle from the dead horse. Damn! That animal had cost him plenty in Deadwood City. He shouldered the load and started walking back. They had only three remounts along and none of them a prize. Hell, could it get any worse? The stinging pain in his back reminded him of his ordeal and of the other danger that still faced them.

Roger broke the silence with a sudden peal of laughter. "At least it wasn't the Nez Percé."

"Injun gal, ain't she?" Jethro speculated as he eyed Rebecca's black braided hair, high cheekbones, and the beaded white elkhide dress.

The three filthy, disheveled blots of humanity stood in a cluster on the far end of the ferry raft, while Lone Wolf and Rebecca Caldwell urged their unwilling mounts on board. Jaspar and his cousins eyed the trim shape of Rebecca's calf and spoke in conspiratorial whispers.

"'Pears so," Jo-Ray decided. "She shore is a purty thang."

"I'd like to get a little o' that," Jethro returned.

"Me, too."

"Too bad that feller's with her," Jaspar lamented.

"Him? Heck-fire, he ain't no bother. Sissy boy or somethin', taking orders from a fe-male. We could fix his arse right easy," Jo-Ray speculated aloud.

"How you mean, Cousin Jo-Ray?" Jaspar asked eagerly.

"Once we git out on that water, he ain't gonna be doin' a lot of walkin' around. One of us could slip up behind him easylike and clonk him over the head. Then, it's over the side and we can have our way with little Missy Two-gun. Long as we keep her away from those horse pistols, there won't be any trouble.

"That shines, Jo-Ray," Jethro said in awe. "You shore is good at figgerin' things, Brother Jo-Ray. Uh . . . which one of us does it?"

"We draw straws."

"Ain't got no straws," Jaspar commented.

"Twigs, then," Jo-Ray snapped impatiently. "Go get three an' break 'em off at different lengths."

Jethro reacted first. He walked past their passengers and onto shore. There he selected three twigs from a cottonwood tree, snapped them at unequal lengths, and returned with his prize tightly clutched in one fist. Jaspar dithered around him like a nervous puppy.

"Well, come on. Draw," Jo-Ray demanded.

Jaspar beamed when he pulled out a short stick. Jo-Ray chortled with excitement when he picked one even shorter. Jethro's face fell. That left him with the longest one.

"Looks like you do it, Brother Jo-Ray."

"Fine with me. Fine as elderberry wine. Save them twigs. We'll need 'em for another draw."

"What for, Cousin Jo-Ray?"

"The gal, dummy, the gal."

"Oh, uh, sure, sure," Jaspar responded vacantly.

"They only got the packhorse to go. Let's get ready to shove off," Jo-Ray commanded.

Icy waters of the Upper Snake River frothed and roiled around the raft as it nudged uncertainly out into the current. Powerful muscles bulged in the dirt-encrusted arms of the three riffraff as they hauled on the towrope. A great sway formed in the hemp cable as the rushing river shoved the raft far downstream, to the northwest. Once passable headway had been achieved against the tug of the water, Jo-Ray left off pulling and hurried aft to check the rear of the vessel.

Acting casual, he started slowly forward, glancing over the side while keeping a close eye on Lone Wolf, who sat on an upended nail keg near the midships line. When Jo-Ray drew closer, he bent down and picked up a wrist-hick oak billet, used for pounding locking pegs into place. He moved swiftly now, arm upraised. A step. Two.

With an audible swish, he brought the heavy wooden club down toward Lone Wolf's head.

"Lone Wolf, look out!" Rebecca shouted.

Too late. Even as the white warrior tried to fling himself to one side, the solid oak slammed down on his head with a terrible clunking sound.

Frozen for the moment by what assuredly had been Lone Wolf's brutal murder, Rebecca roused herself too late. She'd made only two steps toward her snorting mount when Jo-Ray hopped into her path.

"Hurry, boys. It's over the side with him!" Jo-Ray called out even as he jumped between Rebecca and her holstered revolvers athwart her saddle bow.

"No you don't, Missy. No noisy shootin', if you please. Jaspar, bring them twigs. We'll draw again to see who goes first."

Ugly parti-colored eyes fixed on the bulge of Rebecca's breasts. Jo-Ray energetically massaged the large lump in his raggedy trousers.

Chapter 5

Sunlight through the changing alder trees made dappled patterns on the skin of the man beside him. Roger Styles watched the flickering designs for a moment in rapt concentration. A hundred yards from them, in the clearing ahead, graceful, spotted-rump ponies grazed, heads down, in a tableau of tranquility.

"I count only twenty-three horses," Lew Gorce complained in a whisper.

"Same as I have," Roger agreed. "The men must be out. Hunting or visiting, maybe."

"Not tradin' off Appaloosies, I hope," Gorce added.

"We'll have to take what we've got. Do you see any more than those three herd boys?"

"Nope."

"Good. I'll go for the one on this side. You'll have fifteen minutes to get into position for the other two. Pick a good man. Sy Burton'd be my choice. Use knives, or strangle 'em. If we do this quietly, we can get away and no one will be the wiser for a long time. At least I hope we can."

"Hope? Any man who can kill a mad grizzly with an overgrown Arkansas toothpick can do damn near anything he wants to," Gorce returned in sincere compliment.

Despite his hardness and innate viciousness, Roger was touched. "Thanks. I mean that. For a while back there I thought I was dead for sure."

"Hell, Roger, you're too mean to die."

"Enough of you. Get on with it. I want to be well out of this area before dark."

Gorce crawled quietly off into the underbrush, motioning to Sy Burton, and the pair slipped away. In their wake only the humming of drowsy midday insects and the occasional chatter of the Nez Percé boys disturbed the air. Ten minutes slid by leadenly. Tensing himself to respond quickly, Roger started forward.

Eyes fixed on the small, bronze back of a Nez Percé lad of ten or so, Roger moved with easy caution, testing each patch of spongy earth before planting hand or knee. Twenty yards. Still no alarm. He paused and checked the time. Two minutes more. Arms aching from the unfamiliar exercise, his back still a coal bed of pain, Roger covered another fifteen feet. Ten more.

Roger froze as the youngster stood and walked directly toward him. Still screened by the trees, the horse thief was invisible to the boy. Even so, Roger flattened himself and held his breath. The Nez Percé lad stopped beyond the first line of alders, pulled aside his loincloth, and relieved himself in an arching yellow stream, which splattered upon the ground. His personal chore completed, the child remained there, legs astraddle, peering downward as he intently stroked his small, brown penis. Roger flinched as a splatter of Shahaptian words crackled from across the clearing.

"Blue Turtle! Pull it more than five times and you're

49

playing with it!"

All three youngsters laughed shrilly at this witticism. The boy rearranged his breechcloth and turned back to the herd. He settled himself with his back against the smooth bark of an alder. Immediately, Roger began to crawl rapidly forward.

He sensed movement on the far side of the meadow before he actually saw Sy Burton and Lew Gorce rise up and hurl themselves at their intended victims. Without time to even draw his knife, Roger flung himself around the trunk, arms extended.

Clawed fingers closed on the Nez Percé boy's throat and Roger exerted all the strength of his thick arms to squeeze the life from the struggling child. Beads of sweat popped out on his forehead, and he felt a dull ache in the palms of his hands as he increased the pressure.

Distorted by his bulging eyes, the boy's look of pleading registered on Roger's consciousness. The flat-bellied youngster heaved and flopped around in Roger's grasp, tongue protruding thickly from lips retracted by the rictus of straining effort. The smooth, bronze skin of his chest, stomach, and legs rubbed against Roger's bare arms. Suddenly the lad stiffened and began to gurgle.

A trickle of blood ran from one corner of the child's mouth as he involuntarily bit through his tongue. Roger's heart pounded and he began to gasp and moan. With a start he realized that a powerful sexual heat radiated from his loins and he had a rigid, throbbing erection. He gave a final violent heave and panted with relief and satisfaction when he heard the boy's neck snap.

Chest heaving from his effort, Roger laid the body on the ground. Driven by some unexplained compulsion, Roger reached out and gently stroked the boy's slack stomach. A shiver of self-reproach passed through him and he turned away to call softly to Lew.

"Signal the others. We'll round up this lot and head out quickly."

No one pursued them.

Roger knew that for a certainty by four that afternoon. For some reason, the Nez Percé had not sent warriors seeking revenge for the murders and the theft of their horses. Relief flooded him at this realization. Gratitude, too. He had another vexing problem to worry him.

Why was it, he wondered, that as he had strangled the little Nez Percé boy and felt the lad's flesh against his own, he had gotten such a powerful sexual urge? Self-loathing clouded the brightness of their success for Roger Styles.

"I got the short one this time," Jethro gloated as he waved his winning twig under the noses of his brother and cousin. With his other hand he urgently tugged and pulled at the thick bulge in his filth-encrusted trousers.

Rape, Rebecca Caldwell thought. She'd been raped before.

Back when she had first started her vendetta against her worthless uncles, Virgil and Esekial Caldwell, and Bitter Creek Jake Tulley and his gang, she had unwittingly played into Roger Styles's hands. He had stripped her of her clothes and all her defenses, then proceeded to force his will upon her. She fought and he told her how much he enjoyed it when a woman resisted him. She slapped and scratched, and he punched her face and tender breasts until she wailed in agony.

Black-and-blue, wretched with humiliation and defeat, she submitted while he committed the horrible act. She had gotten even, though.

Later, in the buffalo hunting camp maintained by the Tulley Gang, she had nearly kicked his balls off. Although he had managed to escape, she pursued him ever since.

No, Roger Styles would have few peaceful nights, remembering the little half-Sioux girl he had taken his way with. A splash sounded as Jo-Ray and Jaspar heaved Lone Wolf's body over the side. The sound brought Rebecca back to the reality of what was about to happen.

Jethro approached her, fly open, eyes greedy, grime-rimmed mouth working in lewd parody of tender kisses. Well, the boys had voted to kill Lone Wolf and rape her, had they? Not all the votes were in, they would soon find out. Moving carefully, she slid her right hand into the drawstring puckered top of her small beaded possibles bag. The time had come for her to cast her vote.

She did it with her little .38 Smith and Wesson Baby Russian.

"Hike up that dress, sweet thang. You're gonna get some hot meat from ol' Jethro."

The Smith barked once.

Jethro stopped in mid-stride and looked disbelievingly down at his exposed genitals. Numbness radiated out from his groin. He couldn't feel anything. But just for a second there he could swear that little Indian spitfire had shot off one of his balls. Then he saw it laying at his feet.

"Aaaah-yeeee!" A howl of anguish burst from Jethro's lips. He threw back his head and wailed in abject horror at the atrocity that had been committed upon his person. It put Rebecca's aim off slightly and the second .38 slug from her Baby Russian split the point of Jethro's chin and deflected backward to lodge in the root of his tongue.

Jethro staggered and moaned, clutching his savaged genitals while blood gushed through his fingers. Rebecca

52

ignored him to line up on the side of Jaspar's gape-mouthed head.

She put her third round into Jaspar's hairy, dirt-begrimed ear. His eyes bulged and crimson streams burst from his nostrils. With a soft sigh, he slipped over the side and whirled away in the gushing waters of the Snake River. Rebecca came to her feet then, the Smith tracking on Jo-Ray.

Jo-Ray clawed at his waistband, there an antique Colt's Dragoon was held in place by the rope that kept his trousers up. His fingers closed over the use-smoothed grips a moment before Rebecca shot him twice in the right side of his chest. Stunned, he slammed back against the wall of the low ramshackle deckhouse. His revolver forgotten, he sagged to his knees. He cringed at the cold numbness that seeped outward from his gurgling lung and tried to keep the shapely hellion who'd shot him in focus with eyes that blurred and watered.

Rebecca walked toward him. She drew nearer as she deftly snapped open the tilt-top frame of her Baby Russian and ejected the spent cartridges. Competently she fed new fodder to the reliable little Smith, her gaze never leaving Jo-Ray. With all six cylinders loaded this time, she clicked the hinged release in place and eased back the hammer.

"H-how . . . how'd you manage to do that?" Jo-Ray panted out breathlessly.

"You trash were easy. Why, you wouldn't even have been fit to ride with incompetent scum like Jake Tulley and his gang."

"Wh-who's that?"

All the while they spoke, Jethro crawled toward Rebecca, a wide-bladed Sheffield butcher knife in his left hand. His right still clutched his mutilated flesh. Blood ran between his fingers and pumped from his mouth as he made inarticulate noises, mangled by his ruined tongue. Rebecca appeared to ignore him as she answered Jo-Ray.

"Bitter Creek Jake Tulley. He and my low-life uncles traded my mother and me off to the Sioux in exchange for their lives. I lived with the Oglala for five years. About two years ago, I escaped. I started hunting them down."

Jethro had reached a point only a yard from where Rebecca squatted beside the supine Jo-Ray. She interrupted her tale long enough to turn casually and shoot Jethro at a spot precisely centered between his eyes.

Despite the pain in his chest, Jo-Ray gasped and a shudder of cold terror wracked his weakening body.

"Jake and his boys weren't all too bright. Neither were my uncles. But they were mean, vicious, and absolutely without a saving grace. I tracked them, cornered them, and killed them one by one. Only my Uncle Ezekial remains to be punished. None of them were the best riders on the owl hoot trail, but compared to them, you three were pussycats."

Jo-Ray's pallor increased at his sudden knowledge. Oh, what a terrible mistake he and his brother had made. Poor dumb Jaspar had only gone along with it because he'd bragged how easy it would be. Only a little slip of a girl and so hard she could bite nails. Lord, oh Lord, have mercy. Eyes wide with fear, body robbed of all energy, he raised his hands in pitiful appeal.

"W-what are you gonna do now?"

Rebecca gave him a radiant smile as she cocked the Baby Russian and centered its muzzle on the middle of Jo-Ray's forehead.

"Kill you.".

Chapter 6

Made of bark and thatch, much like those of the Eastern tribes—the so-called "Five Civilized Tribes"—the longhouse stood somewhat apart from the rest of the village. Located on the banks of the Clearwater River in Idaho, this band of the Nez Percé enjoyed a serene vista of mountains and plains that soothed the soul. Their headman, Looking Glass, had agreed to host a meeting of the leaders of the four major subgroups. Now his village swarmed with activity as the important persons and their retinues arrived.

First came *Toolhoolhoolzote*, aged misanthrope who rarely had a good word for anything and looked on the world with a face as soured as his disposition. He had been most recent to suffer a loss at his widespread village complex on the Snake River. Next to arrive was *Peopeo Kiskiak Hihi*. Two raids had been conducted against herds of his band. Last to appear was *Hinmahtooyahletkeht*, from the faraway Wallowa Valley in Oregon.

Chief Joseph, as the whites knew him, was tall, handsome, and only thirty-seven years of age, the youngest though most influential of the Nez Percé headmen. Looking Glass welcomed him as an ally in the effort to prevent a general uprising against their unwanted but apparently permanent white neighbors. Over the years, both men had argued persuasively for a policy of forbearance. With the coming of massive horse thievery and murder, that practice wore thin.

"It's good that you're here, old friend," Looking Glass greeted him. "Young *Wahlitits* speaks for war. There are many who agree with him."

"*Toolhoolhoolzote*, of course."

There was no humor in the grim smile the forty-five-year-old chief gave to Joseph. "Naturally. His parents should have named him 'Eats Something Sour.' He can't be faulted all together. Like the other times, some of the children of his band were murdered, horses stolen. White Goose has had two of his villages raided, same thing. Yet he leans to our way of dealing with it."

"The horses are being taken to the west."

"Have you not been raided?"

"No, Looking Glass. The land the whites call Or-e-gon is under white man's law. Stealing horses is against that law, no matter who they are taken from. We have caught sign of the stolen herds. They go to a place called Pen-del-ton. Those who've been wronged should go to the village police in Pen-del-ton, or to the Army."

"*Wahlitits* says they will do nothing."

"Humph." Joseph stood a moment, arms folded across his broad chest. "That's probably true. At least we will have made every effort to do it their way. Who's to blame, then, if our people seek those who do us harm?"

An impish light glowed in Looking Glass's eyes. "You're truly a leader of men. *Hinmahtooyahletkeht.* Perhaps this time the whites would truly hear the 'thunder,' if Thunder Traveling to Loftier Heights were to carry our complaints. Would you do it for us?"

"That's for the council to decide," Joseph responded. "Speaking of which, isn't it about time to get it started?"

"Our shaman is purifying the longhouse now. While he does, we have a welcome feast prepared. Come, enjoy. There's time for strong words later."

Roast bear, broiled salmon, camas bulbs aplenty abounded at the feast. Berries flavored a heady potion that passed from hand to hand around the open fire pit. Everyone ate too much, belched loudly, and ate more. They patted round stomachs and the children went off, droopy-eyed, to doze under the trees or along the river bank. The four principal headmen and representatives of their local councils entered the longhouse.

Wahlitits spoke first. He might have had the gift of reading minds from the angry words that poured from his mouth. "The Army will do nothing. Of all of us, only Looking Glass and his people live on what the whites call our 'reservation.' General Howard's determined to force us all to live here. These whites come now for our horses. Tomorrow it will be our land. There's no end to it. Unless . . . we make an end of it."

Looking Glass looked coldly at the fiery warrior. "We number as the leaves of a tree, yet we're few compared to the whites. Where are the Klamaths? Where are our cousins the Modocs? They fought . . . and they died."

"But these white men have to be stopped!" *Wahlitits* snapped back.

With quiet dignity, Joseph rose. He extended a hand, palm up, to signify he wished to talk. "Before he died, my father told me, 'You must stop your ears whenever you are asked to sign a treaty selling your home. A few years more and white men will be all around you. They have their eyes on this land. My son, never forget my dying words. This country holds your father's body. Never sell the bones of your father and mother.' He believed in a peaceful solution with the whites. That's why he signed the treaty that created this reservation. I also believe in dealing with the white man in a peaceful manner. But what he told me is why I do not choose to live on the reservation.

"The whites have a paper, with writing on it, that says that they, as a people 'are and of a right ought to be free and independent . . .' Is it no less for us? If we remain dignified, calm, present our grievances to the whites in their way, won't they have to accept that we are in our rights?"

"General Howard calls us malcontents," *Wahlitits* scoffed. "He says we must be punished. Perhaps it is he who sends these men to steal our horses, kill our children?"

Joseph thought on it a moment. "No. That is not his way. Six summers ago, white settlers began to move into our valley at Wallowa. At first all went well. Then they began to seize our cattle and horses. They acted as though it were their land. These whites denied us the right to graze our stock or to stay long on ancient campsites, even to fish in the river. Our people were mistreated, some even killed. I refused to allow my warriors to take revenge for these bad things. I believed, as I still do, that we can live side by side with the whites in peace."

"What makes you think that?" *Wahlitits* sneered.

"When our land became part of what the whites call a 'State,' the law stopped white men from stealing our horses and cattle."

"But they didn't stop taking the land, did they?"

Hinmahtooyahletkeht shook his head sadly. "No. They haven't."

"Then I say we must fight! No white man will ever do it for us."

"*Wahlitits*, that way always brings the Army and much bloodshed," Chief Joseph said sadly. "If we do nothing to harm innocent whites and the raids stop, as they always have, we will be left in peace. If we retaliate, the whites won't stop until we've been hunted down and killed to the last man, woman, and child."

"What does the great Thunder Traveling to Loftier Heights propose?"

Chief Joseph ignored the nastiness in *Wahlitits*'s voice. "The white law says a man can defend what is his. We who are vulnerable can herd our horses together in larger number. Put more guards on them, men instead of boys. Let these thieves see if it is as easy to kill warriors."

Mutters of agreement went around the gathered leaders. Old White Goose stood and signed for recognition.

"*Hinmahtooyahletkeht* has spoken wisely. Let us do as he suggests. There will be no more talk of raids on the whites."

All save *Wahlitits* agreed upon this. The proponents of peace had won . . . at least for the moment.

Groaning loudly in protest, the rope cable stretched further downstream. Great. She had taken care of Lone Wolf's killers. Now all she had to do was get off the river. First thing was to get rid of Jo-Ray's body.

She dragged it to the side and kicked the corpse over with one moccasin-clad foot. So much for that. Now she had to pull the raft to the far bank. Rebecca Caldwell strained against the towline, aching in arms and legs, her belly tight and flat. The raft only moved sideways, downstream. Small, froth-flecked wavelets began to splash over the upstream side of the ferry. Rebecca bit at her lower lip and began the struggle again.

A kinking stitch of pain flared up her left side. She fought back stinging tears of agony and planted her feet once more. Another heave on the towrope.

Nothing.

Or at least it seemed like nothing to her. Creaking came from the floorboards and here and there wooden pegs popped out, the ends of decking material springing upward like broken barrel staves. The raft could not take this violent pounding much longer. Gasping, she tried again.

Impossible. Nothing would work. She saw a clear image of the log and plank raft splintering and her body flying out into the harsh, cruel waters. The end loomed in her consciousness.

No! She wouldn't let it defeat her. Think. You know what to do, she chided herself. Something . . . something they tried down in . . . in the Nations. Yes. That was it. Why hadn't she thought of it first?

Horses. So simple. She had three of them. Plenty of power to drive the raft to the far shore. Quickly Rebecca set about rigging a line from the pommel of her saddle horse to the towrope. She eased the nervous animal to the bow of the boat, cinched up the line, and urged the horse to walk toward the stern. Mighty haunches flexed, the roan gelding strained against the power of the tumbling waters.

At first, nothing happened. Another horse, Rebecca

thought in excited concern. No, she rejected the idea. She'd need to use them in relay. She placed one small moccasin-clad foot in the stirrup and swung atop the wall-eyed creature.

"Now, boy. Pull!"

Imperceptively, the ferry moved. Caught precariously in the center of the current, the raft had enormous inertia to overcome. Slowly the deck boards began to slide past under the driving hoofs of the roan. Did she imagine it or did they move faster?

"Harder. That's it . . . pull!"

Five feet of boat had been pulled past Rebecca when she leaped from the saddle and hurried to hitch up Lone Wolf's horse. The pack animal would come last. Again she swung into the saddle and urged the big-chested stallion forward.

"Pull now. Both of you . . . PULL!"

Water sloshed in a steady stream over the side of the raft, running some two inches deep. Big, hard hoofs made wild splashes as the two horses surged against the stubborn current.

Painfully slow, the ferry inched forward.

"More. Hard now."

Rebecca jumped from the saddle and ran to her own mount. "Put your back into it, boy," she begged. "Hard now. Pull."

With a loud, sucking slosh, the raft broke free from the current's enthrallment. It leaped toward the far bank, both horses walking easily now. She wouldn't need the draft horse, Rebecca decided. The tether cable swished in its eyelets, and Rebecca had to rush to the stern to unfasten her horse and lead him back to the bow to do the whole process over again.

"Ho! Ho! Harder, that's it."

It worked. Just like down in Indian Territory. If only Lone Wolf were here to appreciate her ingenuity and to help. A swift knife of grief misted her eyes. She blinked away the tears and looked over her shoulder at the approaching bank.

Only fifty feet. Forty. Twenty-five.

"Pull! Pull! Once more."

She ran frantically from one end of the raft to the other, leading and encouraging the sweating, straining horses. One final heave and the ferry grounded violently against the incline dirt ramp that served as a dock.

Quickly she off-loaded the three animals and secured all the gear. She tied Lone Wolf's mount to the packhorse by its reins and stepped astride her own. With a final glance backward, she wished whatever new proprietor took over the ferry service good luck. Hopefully they'd be of a better stripe than Jo-Ray and his craven partners.

A grim and sorrowful task confronted her. Now she had to search for Lone Wolf's body.

Three spotted-rump ponies waited outside a small cabin. Ground-reined, their heads down grazing on lush green shoots unharmed by the recent summer sun, they waited for their owners. Three children played outside the building. The eldest, *Etaiyamlatit*, a girl of twelve, laughed and ran with her younger brother, Snow Goose. The third youngster, a boy of four, went about entirely naked. His lightly bronzed skin, black eyes, and high cheekbones markedly contrasted with disconcertingly yellow hair. The others called him Ja-mie and he jabbered at them in a mixture of English and Shahaptian. In contrast to their levity, their elders inside the cabin spoke in strained seriousness.

"There is talk of revenge raids. Of killing all whites. I thought you should know," *Taiyan Tanklaal* informed the owner of the cabin.

"Thank you, Buffalo Summer," Thaddius Walsh responded. "It's indeed grave news you bring me. But why should I be worried? I've always been a friend to the *Cho-pun-nish*."

"Yes. And the husband of my sister. Even so, to some of our people you're only another white man. If *Wahlitits* has his way, you'd be in as much danger as any settler. Maybe a little more."

A frown creased Thad's high, smooth brow. "I . . . don't understand. Why would that be?"

"Jamie and 'Liz-bet are considered to be *Cho-pun-nish*. Those who seek to run all whites out of this country will want them returned to the tribe. To do so, they would gladly kill you."

Thad rose from the small hand-built table and strode to the black cast-iron cooking stove. He took a steaming pot from the top surface and returned. After pouring fresh coffee for both of them, he sighed heavily and made a helpless gesture.

"Should we come to Wallowa Valley and live with your people now? I would have to give up all I've struggled to achieve."

"It might be best. Even though two winters have passed, 'Liz-bet is still a baby. Jamie hardly older. The question is, my friend-brother, can you defend what you have here?"

"Alone, you mean?" Thad rubbed a blunt, squarish hand across his brows, obscuring his green eyes for a

63

moment. "I can't answer that. I think so. But then, I don't know what might happen."

"Nor do I. It could be that this talk of war will die of its own weight. *Hinmahtooyahletkeht* spoke strongly in favor of forbearance. Many agreed. For now, there will be no war. Only . . . it's the future I worry about. A few days . . . a Moon from now. I know one thing for certain. If more boys are killed, horses stolen, it'll be impossible to keep some of us young men from fighting the whites."

"You, too, Buffalo Summer?"

Taiyam Tanklaal let his steady gaze slide away from his brother-in-law's probing look. His features, carefully arranged before, slid into a mask of anger. Slowly he nodded.

"It is so. If the whites don't stop, there will be war."

Chapter 7

Fuzzy, indistinct images of leaves and towering tree trunks wavered above. The song of birds and buzzing of insects came muted, as though from miles away. Exhausted by the battle with the river, worn by hours of searching, Rebecca Caldwell lay on the bank and fixed an unfocused stare on the sky. She had ridden and walked for miles along the south bank of the Snake River. Her quest had taken her beyond the big bend. Now she had to admit that her efforts had yielded her nothing.

Her search for Lone Wolf's body had been fruitless. A turmoil of reasons boiled in her head. He had survived somehow. No, that couldn't be. He had been carried to the opposite bank. Possible, but not likely, given the current's flow. He had sunk to the bottom, never to be found.

NO! That she wouldn't allow.

"Lone Wolf . . . ?" A frightened, lonely cry, it came from deep within her, in the voice of a little girl.

They had never been lovers. Lone Wolf followed the sacred way of the Power Road, a medicine quest of the Crow that demanded celibacy. Had they really ever been *happy?* The searching, the killing, the constant struggle to survive against a tough and wily adversary had consumed the months and years they had spent together. What did that leave in its place?

They had been . . . close. Closer than brother and sister, closer than lovers, closer even than twins. Each knew the other's peculiarities and daily routine. Often they entered dangerous, trying situations without the need of discussing individual roles. They traveled well together and fought well. But were they ever happy together?

Rebecca shoved away the unpleasant thoughts. Tears misted her eyes, emblems of a grief that had no words to express itself. She would keep looking. She would not give up. Everywhere she went, she would ask. The loud rumble of her stomach reminded her of the mundane needs of her existence.

Well and good. She would make camp, fix food, sleep. Then she would continue the search tomorrow.

She was young, only fourteen the madam had assured him, and a virgin. He had been frantic with excitement by the time she had been delivered to his door that evening.

"Come in, come in, my dear." Roger Styles invited.

Timidly she entered. Roger closed and secured the portal, then went around the room lowering the kerosene lamps. He wore only a dressing gown. As he had specified, she was dressed as a child some four or five years her junior, with pretty bows in her long, golden hair. He came to her at last and took her small face in his large, hard hands.

"Now, you know why you're here, eh, child?"

The girl nodded. "S-so we c-can have fun together?"

"That's right. What's your name, my little darling?"

"Malissa."

"Oh, that's a fine name, Malissa. I like that. My name's Roger. Miss Jane says that what you mostly do is with your . . . er, your hands and, er-ah, m-mouth. Is that right, Malissa?"

"Y-yes. She . . . she wouldn't let me do anything else, Roger."

"Well, tonight that's all changed. Tonight you become a woman."

Malissa's eyes lit expectantly at that. "Oh, really, Roger, really? I . . . I hear things from the other rooms at Miss Jane's and—and it makes me feel so funny. All squirmy inside. Is it . . . is it really good?"

"Oh, you'll love it. First, though, let me give you a little glass of brandy. It won't hurt. Then, I'll undress you. After that you can show me how much you've learned."

"I'd like that, Roger," Malissa sparkled, deep blue eyes atwinkle.

"Good, Malissa."

Roger gave her the brandy. After she had slowly sipped it, he began to remove each article of her clothing, his breath growing heavier and rougher with every passing moment. At last he had her completely disrobed.

Roger guided her to a chair, where he sat and pulled her down to her knees between his widespread legs. "Now, Malissa dear, show me. Show me everything you've learned at Miss Jane's. And I have something special for you, Malissa," he murmured.

Just when things were getting started, a familiar voice called out, muffled by the thick portal.

"Boss? Roger? Are you in there? This is Lew Gorce.

It's important."

Roger heaved an annoyed sigh.

"I'll be right there," he yelled back.

Roger donned his dressing gown and closed the bedroom door on his way to admit his visitor. He scowled as he looked at Lew Gorce.

"Well? What is it at this time of night?"

"Some of the boys we sent out to scout the herds have come back."

"Come on in and tell me about it."

In the living room, Roger poured brandy for Lew and handed the small balloon glass to his henchman. Roger's eyes shifted in the direction of the bedroom, but all remained quiet. At thought of what waited there, he felt another erection beginning.

"It's like this, Roger. The Nez Percé are rounding up all of their herds. Except for necessary ponies to do work or for hunting, the rest are being grouped in larger herds. They've got warriors guarding them now."

"Hummm. Not so good. Can you get more men?"

"Sure. Easy. Only this makes it a lot harder for us to steal those Appaloosies."

"With more men, more guns, what the hell difference does a few warriors make?" Impatience to get back to the delights of Malissa colored Roger's speech. "The way to look at it is this: Now we get more horses with each raid. How big are these new herds?"

"One numbers over three hundred. It'll take a few days, I suppose. When do you want us to go after them?"

"Gather the boys and leave right away. Find those new men you need. But by all means, get after the horses."

"Can do, Roger. And, uh, enjoy your evening," Lew ended with a wink and a wicked grin.

Roger brightened. "Oh, I will, Lew. I surely will."

With visions of new delights to which he would introduce sweet little Malissa, Roger saw Lew to the door, locked it tightly, and hurried toward the bedroom.

A moment before he entered the bedroom, Roger paused and sighed with regret. Too bad. But it had to be that way. Poor little Malissa would be dead before morning.

Chapter 8

Looking like a bloated orange stigmata, the celestial furnace hung heavily on the distant ridge of hills. Another day had come. Two days since Rebecca Caldwell started her search for the remains of her loyal companion, Lone Wolf. She had not even found a scrap of buckskin nor a sign where predators might have discovered the body and disposed of it for a meal. Rebecca felt defeated.

More so than on that first day when she had given in to grief and self-pity. With a dragging sensation of time too heavy upon her shoulders, she set about her morning breakfast chores. A slight rustle in the brush to her left sent her gaze that direction, while her hand felt into the beaded bag at her waist. A long, tense ten seconds went by, then a lithe young man, dressed in buckskin loin-cloth, leggings, and a bead-decorated hunting shirt stepped out into the small glade.

"What do you do here, woman?" he asked in Shahaptian.

"*Šaielo?*" Rebecca inquired back in Lakota. "Do you speak Cheyenne?" she repeated. "*Lakota yelo?*"

"Ah! *Lakota. he-he.*"

"I am *Šinaskawin* of the Oglala. I came to buy a spotted-rump horse."

"Not buy . . . trade," the young warrior declared in Lakota, eyeing the three horses hobbled for grazing a short ways away.

"All right, trade. What is your name and your people?"

"I am *Hinmahtoo Sahnim*. Fall Thunder in Lakota," the handsome young brave told her in poorly accented, childlike Lakota. "My people are the *Cho-pun-nish*. The Nez Percé. Our village is short ways, on river. Will you come?"

"Yes, of course. Have you . . . has anyone in your village seen a man's body in the last few days? A drowned man? Tall, yellow hair, wore the clothes of the Crow tribe?"

Fall Thunder needn't look thoughtful. "No. We have not seen such an odd thing. He was a friend?"

Water filled Rebecca's eyes. "A very good friend. White men killed him on the river to the south of here."

"Bad men those," Fall Thunder remarked, brow puckered with remembering. "Where are they now?"

"In the black pit."

Fall Thunder made a face of happiness. He smiled whitely. "Your friend . . . he fought them? Killed them?"

"No. I did. They had no honor, so I did not take their hair, as is the Dakota custom."

An odd expression came on Fall Thunder's face. A woman fighting, killing three bad men like those with the box that crossed water? He could not keep his skepticism from showing.

"It's true, all the same. I finished them off and fed their bodies to the fishes."

71

"It is good anyway it happened. All whites are bad."

"I'm not going to argue that point now. Help me load my camp gear and we will go to your village."

"A man . . . help with a woman's work?"

"There are only two of us," Rebecca told him testily.

"So? What's that have to do with it?"

"Oooh! Dammit. Men are the same anywhere. *I'll* load up, you show the way."

"That's good. Right way for man, woman to do their jobs."

"Gawd! There's more than three hundred horses here," Sy Burton blurted in a hushed voice.

"They've added from other villages," Lew Gorce remarked on the obvious.

"All the better for us," Clem Dye gloated.

"I don't like this," Niel Thorne complained as he crawled up to the observation point. "I was over on the other side. Me'n the boys saw maybe a dozen warriors watchin' the herd along with the kids."

"You were supposed to stay the hell on the other side," Lew told him coldly. "We knew about the warriors from the fellers who found this herd. No surprises there. Now go do as you were told, or find another outfit."

"Uh . . . I'm sorry, Lew."

"That's right. You're damned sorry. Only try to rise above it. Go on, we'll hit them about noontime when they've got their hands full of grub."

Noon came faster than most of the rustlers expected it. Cook fires had been lighted in the herd camp and the stomach-teasing aroma of roasting meat filled the air. Lew made a final check of his men and retreated from his lookout to mount his horse.

"We might as well do it," he observed. "Long as the boys keep to that half circle we can drive the Appaloosies and their guards along ahead of us. I'm going over to be in the center," he told Sy. "Make sure you keep this wing in line."

"You bet, Lew. Nothin' to it."

"You'll think that when you run face first into an alder. Five minutes. Then, when you hear my first shot, everyone moves."

"Can you trust that whelp, Thorne, to carry his end?"

"Nope. That's why I sent Clem along." Lew favored Sy with a brief grin, then walked his mount away through the thick grove of alder and ash.

From his pivotal position at the center of the crescent formation, Lew Gorce took careful aim at a mature warrior who sat astride a magnificent specimen of the Palouse horse. His finger took up slack on the Winchester's trigger and he sensed the fall of the hammer.

Smoke and flame erupted from the muzzle and a 205 grain bullet sped toward the target. Immediately, more shots sounded and, with wild whoops, the outlaws moved in on the herd. Lew saw his men move in with satisfaction as the big brave jerked backward and fell from his mount. Nez Percé boys yelled shrilly and raced for whatever weapons they had along.

Taken by surprise, the warriors among the herd guards snatched up their arms and fired blindly at unseen targets. The unfettered ponies whirled in confusion and added choking dust to the tumult of the moment. With a wild trumpeting of command, one stallion took the lead, drawing the herd away from the danger at sides and rear.

Lew's plan worked excellently so far. He howled like a tormented soul and fired his rifle into the air.

"At 'em boys! Keep 'em movin'."

A youngster of thirteen or fourteen leaped up from the tall grass and fired an arrow. Lew watched the arc of its travel. He couldn't help the small smile of relief when the barbed projectile buried itself in Niel Thorne's chest.

Thorne dropped his rifle and clutched frantically at the object which brought such pain to his body. Bloody froth appeared on his lips and he began to whine in terror. Lost to the present, it brought him no compensation when Lew Gorce shot the Nez Percé boy in the side of the head a moment after the arrow had struck. The frantic clawing of Thorne's fingers slowed, then ceased, as the youthful bandit slid from the saddle and disappeared into the tall grass. Lew looked around for a new target.

"Sy!" he yelled over the thunder of hoofs. "Don't let those Injuns turn the herd. Blast 'em!"

Caught in enfiladed fire, the warriors streaked away, turning behind the galloping rustlers. For a moment, Lew felt relief, then he realized that they now had their enemy at their backs. His mind began feverish replanning.

"Ride like hell!" he wanted to yell.

Those redskin bastards were behind them. Would they take advantage of it and attack at once? He hoped not. The previous night, Clem and Sy had helped him prepare a nasty surprise for anyone who pursued them. Lew's original plan banked on keeping the enemy close until the driven herd reached a certain spot. Yeah, but not too close. How would he guarantee that?

Lew fired his Winchester into the air. "Pick it up! Get 'em goin'."

Mounted now, the herd boys fought to break the circle

74

of men and provide a route of escape for themselves and the horses. One of them crashed the breast of his spotted-rump pony into the side of Red Ashton's mount.

"Sonofabitch!" Red bellowed. He swung sideways with the seven-inch barrel of the Army-model Colt he fisted in his right hand.

The right side of the boy's head caved in with a crunch of shattered bone. It oddly distorted the shape, bulging his eyes, giving the youth a lopsided appearance. Blood ran from his nose and ears, and the dead boy fell from his pony. Only another mile, Lew thought as he rode past the small corpse.

Hit and run and hit again. The tactics of the Plains Indians, adapted to forest land, worked well for the Nez Percé. At least against the enemies they usually fought. These whites who came to steal their horses didn't follow the expected form of battle. In fact, they only fought when someone got in their way. Big Stone mulled over this discovery as he led the warriors in pursuit of the fleeing rustlers.

"It is strange," he shouted to Bear Heart, who rode beside him.

"What is that?"

"These whites seem only to want our horses. They don't stand and fight."

A bleak smile curved Bear Heart's mouth. "Be glad of that, Big Stone. They have many guns. They could kill us all."

"Are you afraid to die?"

"No. Only of dying *uselessly*."

"Then let's take the fight to them and die doing

something useful."

"You men I named off, dismount. The rest of you keep the herd moving," Lew Gorce commanded.

"How long do you figger we've got?" Red Ashton demanded.

"Two minutes . . . if we're lucky."

"You'd better get to doing something, then."

"Stopper that mouth, Red," Lew growled. "We want to suck 'em way into this defile first. To do that we've got to make 'em think they can win."

"Sounds damned dangerous to me."

"So's crossin' the road when the stage is comin'. Quit the gripin' and take your position."

A minute and a half later, the first warriors raced into the narrow pass that divided their homelands from that of neighboring bands. Rifles and six-guns crackled to life. Surprised by this sudden change in tactics, Big Stone tried to make his men wheel and retreat.

Too late.

Small spurts of blue-white smoke showed along the steep rock walls and across the trail in front of them. Nez Percé braves milled in confusion and fired at the flashes of the white men's guns. Almost at once the puffs of smoke disappeared.

Twenty-five sticks of dynamite went off as one.

A horrendous roar filled the pass. Chips of rock flew about like shrapnel. Horses screamed and men howled in agony. Blinded and choked by dust, the Nez Percé pulled back. Behind them, they left six more dead and three dying.

Bitterness painted their faces as they listened to the

triumphant whoops and yells of their enemy. A short distance away, *Wahlitits* and four of his loyal followers sat watching the destruction.

"We must hold another war council," he advised in bitter tones. "The day of reckoning must come soon."

"The whites want everything!" *Wahlitits* exploded amid a jumble of contending voices. "If not this year, then the next, or the one after that. They must be driven from our land. More men and boys died yesterday. More of the people's horses were stolen. Yet there is still talk of peace. I spit on peace!"

"You are a brave man, *Wahlitits*," White Goose said calmly. "No one doubts that. You fight with the courage of ten and the skill of twice that number. Yet, your anger clouds your judgment. We must try to the end of our days to have peace. Because . . . we're as nothing to the white man."

"Because he thinks us inferior," *Wahlitits* snapped.

"There's that, of course. Also, because we cannot enter into battle in the same way as the whites, that's what I was speaking about. Although we are many, we're not strong enough to match the whites in the way that most counts. We are like the leaves that change color in this time of *Sahnim* then fall from the trees to not be seen there again. Not until *Etaiyam* do new buds swell the branches. For us to make a protracted war is not possible."

"What is the meaning of your fable, old man?"

White Goose gave the young warrior a patronizing smile. "When a warrior falls in battle, we cannot replace him in time. Not in a day, or a Moon, or a season. The whites number like the blades of grass. When we cut down one, ten more spring up to take his place. This they can do in a day. Were we to try our strength against such a self-renewing enemy, we would not last to the coming of *Enim*, let alone until next Spring."

"Then I still say we must fight!"

"How would we do this?" Looking Glass asked politely. "What could be acomplished by killing and burning out innocent settlers?"

"If we kill enough, leaving some alive, those who are spared can become messengers for us. Charge them to tell their brothers that the raids will go on until the guilty ones are brought to us for their just punishment. Surely, to save their own kind, they will act on our demands."

White Goose spoke through a heavy sigh. "I truly wish it would be that way. But to do such to the white man would only bring down his hottest anger upon us. Win or lose it would be the same for us. From where I stand, I say this: To take such a warpath would be to make all the *Cho-pun-nish* as a puff of smoke, to rise bravely, thin, and at last disappear in the wind. None would remember our names."

Red-faced, *Wahlitits* stamped the ground angrily. "Then so be it! War! I say it is war!"

The voting sticks went around, red end or blue, and again *Wahlitits* failed to win the council's confidence. To their disappointment, though, Looking Glass and White Goose noticed that even in defeat, *Wahlitits* had more of the council accepting the necessity of the warpath than before.

Chapter 9

"A stranger has come! A stranger has come! She seeks horses. Who will trade horses?" the camp herald declared as Fall Thunder escorted Rebecca Caldwell into the Clearwater River encampments of the Nez Percé.

Women and children turned out, curious about a woman alone seeking their beautiful horses. Surely there was a mistake. She had beauty, though. All could see that. Straight of back, her braided black tresses hanging below her shoulders, straight nose, full, lush lips below high cheekbones and forehead. But those eyes! Startlingly sky-blue. How could that be? For her own part, Rebecca took in the Nez Percé.

Handsome. All of them. The men tall and slim, smooth-limbed and well-muscled. The youths still good-looking and apparently lacking much of the awkwardness of teenage years. The women beautiful, skin clear and glowing, eyes bright and eager, heads and limbs nicely shaped, like their men. The children she found precious. Rebecca wanted to lift and hug them in bunches, like flowers. Shoe-button eyes sparkled. Smiling, happy faces upturned toward her. Most of those under ten or so ran naked through the first village they entered. Their bodies glowed with health. What a truly gorgeous people. No glowed with health. What a truly gorgeous people. No wonder they raised such magnificent horses. In the center village, they stopped before a large bark and thatch longhouse.

"You are welcome among our people, daughter of the Dakota," Looking Glass declared, filling the role of host. "Although you come in a troubled time."

"I am sorry that my visit finds you distressed," Rebecca answered in Lakota. Beside her, *Hinmatoo Sahnim* translated.

"It is not of your doing. White men are stealing our fine horses."

Rebecca frowned. "Have many of yours been stolen?"

"Not among the Clearwater people. Other bands of the *Cho-pun-nish* have suffered. Men and children murdered, horses stolen."

"When did this begin?"

"A Moon ago. Last time *Toolhoolhoolzote's* villages lost many ponies. Three tens, times ten hands were driven away by white men."

"Do you know where they are taken?"

Looking Glass scowled momentarily. This was man's talk, not the province of women. Even so, something about the young Oglala girl made him trust her, want to confide, and perhaps learn some answers. He shrugged.

"To a white village called Pen-del-ton."

"Isn't that in Oregon?" Rebecca inquired.

"Yes."

"Oregon's a state. They have laws to protect you from such things."

"This is as *Hinmahtooyahletkeht* says. Some of our men speak of war."

"A war would be disastrous. It would bring down

frightful retaliation from the Army. I have lived among the whites and I know. Perhaps there is some way I can learn what is behind this." Looking Glass's frown transmitted his doubt.

"In the proper clothes, I can look very much like a white woman," Rebecca insisted. "I could go to Pendleton and find out."

"You look good as you are," Looking Glass told her with a grin. "What you propose must be discussed. There's no feast for a visiting woman, but there is for horse traders. Also the headmen of most bands are here. Tonight we feast them. We feast you, too."

"That's very kind of you, Looking Glass. Thank you. I'll be delighted."

"After we eat, men talk of your ideas. If they are good, you can help us. Until then, my lodge is yours. My daughter will be your host and serve you." Looking Glass raised his voice. *"Etaiyamlatit!* Come here, daughter."

A slim, attractive girl of fourteen or so bent low to pass through the doorway of the longhouse. She walked with fluid coordination, swaying gracefully. Her hair, combed to a lustrous blue-tinged black and secured in shell-decorated gathers over each ear, accented the sweetness of her features and fairness of her skin. Her dark eyes glowed with excitement.

"This is Spring Flower," Looking Glass introduced. *"Etaiyamlatit,* this is a Dakota girl called *Šinaskawin*. Show her the hospitality of our home."

"Yes, father. I'll be glad to do so. *Šinaskawin*. What does that mean in Shahaptian?"

"White Robe Woman," the translator supplied.

"Oh, how pretty. I see . . . the sacred white buffalo of the Dakota people, right?"

81

Rebecca flushed slightly. "That's what it's supposed to be. My father gave it to me."

"He is a wise man. Now, you will want to put away your things, take a bath, and put on pretty clothes. Isn't it wonderful you came on a feast day?"

Chattering away, Spring Flower led Rebecca from the front of the lodge.

"Go on, Magpie," Looking Glass called fondly after her. "Show *Sinaskawin* the womanly things. We will see our guest at the feast."

Unlike the quiet pockets of the shallow creeks on the Great Plains, the rock-lined pool of the women's bathing place on the Clearwater River captured some of the lively stream's turbulence. It swirled with all the appearance of a whirlpool, froth tipping the undulating eddy. Spring Flower brought Rebecca there and, by signs, indicated they were to bathe in this spinning freshet.

Rebecca nodded and smiled, then began to remove her clothing. A hesitant moment later, Spring Flower did the same.

"It is my second bath today," Spring Flower told her in Shahaptian.

"Yes. This *is* a lovely place for bathing," Rebecca replied in Lakota.

Spring Flower's puzzled smile turned into a giggle. "*Sinaskawin*, I don't know what you say and you don't know what I'm saying. Yet, already we are good friends. I . . . feel it."

Paler bronze skin revealed itself as Spring Flower removed her single simple garment. She smiled again and dimples appeared.

"You're really quite a beautiful girl," Rebecca remarked of her companion.

Etaiyamlatit giggled again, then gasped when Rebecca removed her beaded elkhide dress. She had never seen someone so few years older than she who had such a lovely, ripe form. No sign of going to fat evidenced itself on *Šinaskawin*. Not like the women of her people. Muscles rippled under the golden skin. Her breasts, though not large, were full and firm. Unbidden, Spring Flower's eyes took in other details: the narrow waist; wide, womanly hips; long, strong legs. The sight made Spring Flower tremble slightly. Some day she would look like that. The realization excited her.

"The water is cold," she informed Rebecca in a hushed voice. Beckoning to her guest, she stepped out into the swirling stream.

Rebecca followed. "This water is sure cold," Rebecca exclaimed in Lakota.

Abruptly, she arched her lovely form and dived under the surface. Squealing at thought of the chill water, Spring Flower did likewise.

The fourteen-year-old swam like a natural creature of the deep. In the clear, cold of the river, her shapely limbs took on even more grace. She quickly caught up to where Rebecca had surfaced, standing on the smooth rock bottom.

From a great distance could be heard the irregular thumps of almost-thunder. Faintly she thought she heard screams. Then, from closer at hand, a voice cried out. "The horses! They're after the horses!"

Although Rebecca didn't understand the words, Spring Flower did. The girl stiffened and signed the symbols for "raiders" and "horses."

Instantly, Rebecca struck out for the bank. Still gleamingly wet, she shrugged into her elkhide dress and

83

moccasins and rushed toward the camp. A number of warriors, Fall Thunder among them, clutched weapons and ran to gather in their ponies from in front of the lodges. Rebecca's horse remained tethered outside the longhouse and she ran directly to it. She swung into the saddle and loosened the Smith Americans in their holsters.

"Where?" she demanded.

Urgency and action made her meaning clear, and several *Cho-pun-nish* warriors pointed the direction before *Hinmatoo Sahnim* could translate. Rebecca nodded and kicked her mount into a gallop. In the midst of the shouting young men, she rode to rescue the spotted-rump ponies.

Bullets snapped and cracked through the trees above their heads, to be answered by the haunting moan of arrows in flight. The horses had been driven through a narrow defile that led to lower ground to the west of the river. Seven white men had taken cover at the mouth of this ravine. They fired rapidly at their pursuers, keeping them from getting off the higher plateau. Reinforcements arrived for the *Cho-pun-nish* herd guards and the outlaws thought little of it.

Then the return fire of the Indians changed drastically. Added to the hum of arrows, which they paid little attention to at that range, came the heavy roar of a revolver. It fractured the air, and the crack of close-placed bullets made the horse thieves duck their heads. In the same moment, the Nez Percé braves charged. In their midst came what appeared to be a young squaw.

Consternation froze the hard cases for a moment when

they saw that it was she who held the long-barreled .44 Smith and Wesson. Flame and smoke bloomed from her right hand and they discovered she shot with astonishing accuracy.

Rock chips from a ricochet slashed into the face of one gunhawk and he howled in anguish, hands pressed to his bleeding cheeks. From one eye socket, a blackish fluid trickled over his fingers. Hurting too badly for it to register, he had yet to discover he had been partially blinded.

"Let's get out of here!" a voice yelled in English.

"Throw down your guns!" Rebecca shouted back. "Give up and you won't be harmed."

"T'hell with that!" another pistolero boomed.

Rebecca's Smith American spoke again.

Hot lead from the .44 Smith smacked into the gunman's side. Rebecca shot him again, shattering his right elbow.

Bleating yelps of pain and fear came from the defiant one as he rose from the protection of a boulder. Instantly his chest sprouted three feathered appendages. His screams turned to gurgles, and he lurched forward to drape his body in a wet, red smear on the huge rock.

"Pull back! Pull back!" the frantic voice of Clem Dye screeched.

"Wait! Wait for me. I'm blinded! Oh Jesus God, I'm blind. I'm blind!" the man with the rock-scoured face wailed in horror.

Close enough now for lance work, the *Cho-pun-nish* warriors swarmed in among the fleeing white men. Wickedly hooked barbs on the leaf-shaped blades of their war lances sawed through flesh, leaving agonizing trails of fire and blood. The rustlers of the rear guard staggered and reeled about in confusion. At last Clem Dye found his horse and those of three others.

"Come on. Let's get away from here," he commanded.

Fighting for their lives every inch of the short distance to the horses, the surviving outlaws strove to make good their escape. One of their number shrieked hideously as Fall Thunder sank his serrated lance tip in the gunman's vitals. His terrible clamor cut off abruptly when Rebecca's Smith .44 belched flame again.

Rebecca holstered her first revolver and drew the next. She didn't regret the mercy shot as she watched the survivors make hasty retreat down the gully toward lower ground and the safety of their companions. Rebecca sent three bullets after them for good measure. Then she looked around and saw only Nez Percé warriors standing in the settling dust.

With the same suddenness that began it, the fighting ended.

"*Wahlitits* is right, we must go to war," an angry young brave declared.

Firelight flickered off the war-painted body of the speaker. He stood in a pose of righteous anger, arms folded over his bare chest, eyes aglitter with the lust for revenge. Beyond him, the Idaho darkness seemed unrelieved on a moonless night.

Evening had come and with it another council meeting. This time every man in the clan villages had been summoned.

"Yes." "Yes!" Agreement went around the circle.

"Now the whites even come to steal our horses from this ground that their treaty gave us. There is no law for the *Cho-pun-nish* except the strength of our arms and the sharpness of our weapons," he went on passionately. "I say we fight."

Looking Glass raised a hand for silence. "This is a grave matter my brother, Walking Horse, speaks of. We alone can't decide for war. It must be approved by every band of the *Cho-pun-nish.*"

"The headmen are here, let them decide now," Walking Horse challenged.

"*Hinmahtooyahletkeht* isn't here," Looking Glass replied calmly. "We have sent for him. When we know his heart, and those of his people, then we can decide."

"Why do we need him? He will only speak for keeping the peace. *He* does not live on the reservation, yet he says we must follow the white man's law. His words are hollow like a gourd in the Moon of *Hoplal.*"

"It is our way, Walking Horse," Looking Glass explained patiently. "You know that as well as any of us. He has sent word he will be here in two days. Meanwhile, let's not speak more of war. A small boy was killed today, and three of our warriors. Let us mourn for them and tell stories of their greatness while among us."

A slow throb of drums began and a tightness grew in Rebecca's throat. Eyes distant, lost on images of the past, she thought of the many whom she knew closely who had died during the long years of her search for vengeance.

Chapter 10

"Three hundred sixty-seven . . . three hundred sixty-nine . . . three hundred seventy, uh, four. By jove, Roger, that gives us nearly five hundred head on hand. Marvelous old boy," Clive Reversford burbled when he finished counting. "Your chaps are doing a remarkable job."

"And losing a few of their number every time. Those Nez Percé are getting smart."

"What matter that, eh, old boy?"

"I'll tell you what matter. It's hell on morale. Some of the boys are talking about moving on. They don't like the prospect of dying with some savage's bone spear shoved in their guts. Frankly, I don't blame them."

Reversford waved a hand around at the corrals and the steadily growing community of Pendleton. "You don't seriously contemplate quitting now, do you?"

"Of course not," Roger snapped back. "Only I need to have a source of more men. Also, it would look good to the ones left if you were to come on the next raid."

"I?" Clive Reversford fiddled nervously at his lacy cravat. "Why, that's out of the question, old boy. Me? You know I abominate sleeping on the ground, eating grit in my food, the stench of horses. Whew! Absolutely out of the question."

"Clive," Roger said menacingly. "Either you go . . ."

"Or what, Roger? Surely you're not threatening a partner in crime, are you?"

"I don't threaten. Anything I say, I tend to carry out." Reversford's usually foppish drawl turned steely. "And what, pray, were you about to say?"

Roger studied the younger man standing at the corral rail. Clive Reversford's ordinary slouch had stiffened into a martial attitude of attention. His jawline had firmed and the eyes narrowed to slits. Roger thought he knew Clive, had become aware of every nuance of his wastrel's pose. This new facet gave Roger pause, compelling him to moderate his anger.

"That if you did not come on the next raid, as I intend to do, you could spend your next few weeks along the docks in Seattle and other dingy ports recruiting a new crop of hard-nosed bastards, who can stay atop a horse and drive half-wild ones here to us. Also to warn you that if the supply dries up, you'll find yourself, like the rest of us, severely limited in the amount of profit you can expect."

Harsh reality drained Clive Reversford of his new-found bravado. His features melted back into their usual expression of insipid boredom. He toyed again with his cravat, flicked imaginary dust from his lapel, and took a deep breath.

"Well . . . er, ah . . . yes. You've come upon a nasty little conundrum there, haven't you? It seems that I, ah, may have to take drastic measures to insure a steady flow of profit. There surely must be some sort of outfitter here in Pendleton who can provide the necessary equipment to make camp life endurable. I suppose I should pop off and find him, what?" Reversford started for the street, then did a dramatic pause and turn. "That is, if it's still on for our going into the bush, eh, old boy?"

Roger shook his head sadly. "You are impossible, Clive. Now get the hell out of here."

Clive departed hastily, headed toward his lodgings on the opposite edge of town. Lew Gorce shouldered past the young Englishman, a worried expression on his face. He greeted Roger perfunctorily and only nodded thanks to the praise given for the big haul.

"Roger, there's something strange happened out there. I don't know what to make of it."

"How's that, Lew?"

"On that second herd we went after—just a small one, but easy to get to—we ran into the stiffest resistance so far. The funny part, though, an' I don't mean ha-ha funny, there was a squaw fightin' with those braves. She come blazin' in there with a pair of big Smith revolvers."

A touch of cold seeped along Roger's spine. Many tribes had warrior women, he had heard. It couldn't be possible. No. The icy snake spread outward to clutch at his heart.

"Wha-what did she look like?"

"I didn't get close enough to her to tell. Clem says she was somethin', though. A real looker. Young, and not a bit ugly." Lew paused, recalling the description Clem had given after the rear guard escaped from the Nez Percé.

"She rode a white man's saddle, with a pair of old horse pistol holsters over the pommel. An' Clem said she dressed different than the other Injuns. Wore a white dress with beads on it. More like the Sioux than the Nez Percé."

Every word drove another frigid sliver of apprehension through Roger's chest. He swallowed with difficulty and licked his lips.

"Her eyes. What color were her eyes?"

"Uh . . . you got some notion who this gal was?" Lew inquired.

"Ah . . . no. Not really," Roger lied. He thought he new only too well who she might be.

"Well, Clem never saw her eyes. So I can't say on that. Brown, most likely. Like the rest of the savages."

"I'm not too sure," Roger said mostly to himself.

Here? Rebecca Caldwell here? How could she possibly know? The frightened questions clamored unheard and unanswered in Roger's head.

"He has come! *Hinmahtooyahletkeht* has come with two hands of his warriors," the camp crier announced in a leather-lunged shout.

Twenty warriors. It could mean that his heart had changed to favor war. The speculation went around the camp. Her status changed by the fight against the rustlers, Rebecca Caldwell stood with Looking Glass and his council to greet the new arrivals. Her curiosity had been aroused by stories of the headman of Wallowa Valley, the one the whites called Chief Joseph.

What a handsome man! Younger than she had expected, Rebecca admitted to herself as Joseph and his retinue approached the longhouse. His remarkable good looks and calm bearing inspired confidence and affection. A disquieting tremor began in Rebecca's loins, which she quickly suppressed. Near the center of the procession rode a prisoner, closely guarded, veiled in dust.

When the visitors halted and a light breeze blew away

the obscuring cloud of brown particles, Rebecca's eyes widened with shocked disbelief, tears springing to them as the two headmen greeted each other warmly. Chief Joseph's words, though spoken from only a few feet away, seemed to echo with great distance.

"We found this white man on the trail to your lodges. He must be one of the ones who steal our horses."

Roughly, two warriors dragged the partly clad man from his horse. His eyes seemed blank and unknowing. Features slack, like an idiot's gape, he gazed disinterestedly at the surrounding people. At a sign from *Hinmahtooyahletkeht*, the braves half dragged the prisoner forward.

"No!" Rebecca shouted in English. "It's Lone Wolf!"

She turned to Looking Glass, arms extended in passionate appeal. "He is not one of your enemies. He . . . he's my friend. His name is Lone Wolf," she explained in rapid, emotion-charged Lakota.

Fall Thunder fell far behind in his translation. Frustrated for the moment, Rebecca turned on the men who held onto Lone Wolf.

"Let him go!" she demanded. "He's more than he seems. Much more."

"How is this? A woman speaks as one of the council?" Joseph inquired of his friend.

"She is a warrior-woman of the Dakota," Looking Glass responded, making the universal throat-slashing sign for the Sioux. "She helped us fight the whites when they came for horses."

"Who does she say this man is?"

"Lone Wolf," Fall Thunder replied in Shahaptian.

"He's a Crow warrior," Rebecca blurted out. "At least he used to be. He's been my friend and companion since I left the Oglala. He is on your side, just as I am." Face pained with impatience and concern, Rebecca turned to Lone Wolf.

"Brett . . . Brett . . . are you . . . all right?"

"Wha . . . ?" came an empty reply.

"You are Brett Baylor . . . Lone Wolf of the *Absaroka*. I'm Becky. *Sinaskawin* of the Oglala, don't you know me?" Rebecca kept her voice low, controlled, though she wanted to shout.

"Huh? Who? Who am I?"

"*Brett Baylor*, dammit! Lone Wolf, oh, listen to me. I'm Rebecca Caldwell. We were on our way here to get Palouse horses. You were hit on the head, thrown off that ferry over the Snake River."

"Unnh!" A fleeting light of remembering flickered in Lone Wolf's eyes, then died.

Tears welled under Rebecca's lashes and she fought them back. "Where have you been? Lone Wolf, *listen to me!*"

"I, uh . . . I, uh . . . water. Woke up in water. How did I get there?"

"Those men. Jo-Ray and the other two. They attacked you, tried to have their way with me. You went into the river, oh, a week ago. Where were you all this time?"

A white grin flashed on Lone Wolf's face as disarranged synapses flashed anew. "How bad did you hurt them?"

"I killed all three. Oh, you do remember. Oh, thank God. Thank the Great Spirit. Do you know me now?"

"Uh . . . you're . . . uh . . . B-B-B-Becky. Uh . . . I . . ."

"Think!" She shouted it.

"Bu-Bu-Brett . . . Baylor? You said Brett Baylor. But, I'm . . . I'm L-L-Lone Wolf." He looked around him at the wide, dark faces. "Everyone in the village knows me. I

93

fought Turtle Hand to win my place with the *Absaroka*. I am one of you now. I am your brother, Lone Wolf."

A terrible pang assailed Rebecca. The blow on his head and exposure to the elements had addled Lone Wolf's mind. He thought himself to be back among the Crow tribe. Again, she wanted to weep, forcefully rejected the weakening emotion, and tried once more.

"We are in Idaho. These are the *Cho-pun-nish*, the Nez Percé." Helplessly, she turned to Looking Glass. "This is the man I spoke of before. The one who came with me. He is . . ."

Looking Glass, who had remained silent until now, interrupted with a raised hand. "We believed you the first time, daughter of the Oglala. Do not fear for his life. I didn't follow the words you spoke in the language of the whites, but I can see what is there to be seen. He is welcome. It seems his mind is sick, more than his body. Our shaman can help him."

Relief gushed through Rebecca's taut being. She blinked back the insistent moisture in her eyes and summoned a fleeting smile.

"I am grateful."

"You are a Dakota woman?" *Hinmahtooyahletkeht* inquired in good, though accented English.

"Yes. I am half Oglala. My father was Iron Claw of the Beaver Lodge Hoop. My mother a white woman named Hannah Caldwell. Lone Wolf has been my friend and companion for more than two years. After the white men at the river attacked us, I lost contact with Lone Wolf. I am so relieved that you found him. Thank you."

"There are herbs to give forgetting sleep, to soothe and revive the mind. Looking Glass has a good shaman. Let him work his medicine on your friend."

"I . . . yes, I think that best."

"You are the warrior woman I was summoned to meet?"

"I am. You have brought many warriors. Is your mind now set to fight?"

Joseph shook his head. "No. I still seek to walk the path of peace. These," Joseph made a gesture to include his company of warriors, "are for protection. When whites raid even onto our *reservation*," he made the word sound like something slimily obscene, "it is wise to be able to defend oneself."

"I understand. *Hinmahtooyahletkeht*, it would be disastrous to enter into open warfare with the whites. From what Looking Glass tells me, you feel the same. I know he does. I have offered to go to Pendleton and look into what the whites are doing. Find out why they are stealing so many of your horses. With your influence along with your friends, Looking Glass and old White Goose, I'm sure something could be accomplished this way."

"Such as?"

"Once it is established why and by whom these thefts are being done, an appeal can be made to the authorities. Something can be done."

"You are sure you can deal with the whites as an equal?"

"Why not? My mother was of their people. And I have resources that I can draw upon. Money greases the ways when it comes to dealing with politicians." Rebecca smiled coyly.

"You're an astute person, *Šinaskawin*. I am inclined to try your way. The council will meet and we will let you know. Now, let Lone Wolf of the *Absaroka* rest and recover his spirit. While he does, we'll debate. Then . . . it is in the hands of the Great Spirit."

"It will be as you say, *Hinmahtooyahletkeht*," Rebecca acquiesced.

Two days of feasting and emotion-charged council meetings followed. During that time the shaman of the Clearwater band danced and chanted over the supine form of Lone Wolf. Drugged by the medicine herbs the doctor administered, he remained in a state of semiconsciousness during the involved procedure. On the morning of the third day, he awakened clear-eyed and calm.

"How did I get here?" he asked in a close likeness of his usual strong, bass voice.

"*Hinmahtooyahletkeht* of the Wallowa Valley band brought you," the shaman replied through Fall Buffalo's translation.

"Then . . . where is *here?*"

"You are on the Clearwater River."

"Is Rebecca Caldwell here? The woman called *Sinaskawin*, a Dakota?"

"Yes. This is her lodge you rest in. She is the one who made you known to us, Lone Wolf of the far-off *Absaroka.*"

"Where is she?"

"I have sent a boy to find her," was all the reply the old medicine man gave.

Rebecca arrived filled with excitement. "Is it true?"

"Is what true? That I've gotten tired of sleeping all the time? That's for certain. I'm still fuzzy. One of those river rats slugged me with something. The next thing I know, I was wandering on the south bank of the Snake. Far below the big bend. Then, I . . . uh! Everything goes blank."

"We'll probably never know what all happened."

"I seem to remember you telling me you finished off all three of them."

"Yes. When Chief Joseph first brought you here, I told you so. I shot them all and threw them to the fishes."

"Good riddance. What do we do now?"

"Trade for Palouse horses and help these people. Someone is killing their young men and boys and stealing large numbers of their ponies."

"Where do we go and how long do we have?"

Rebecca smiled warmly. "You're back to normal, Lone Wolf. That's for sure. I, uh, can't answer your second question. As to where, it's Pendleton, Oregon."

"Hummm. Any ideas?"

"None."

"We'll learn soon enough."

"Of course. Ah . . . are you, uh, feeling all right?"

"Weak, naturally. And hungry. Don't they feed guests around here?"

"I'll get you something. Oh, I'm so glad you came out of it all right." Impulsively, Rebecca leaned down and gave Lone Wolf a chaste kiss on his forehead.

At mid-afternoon, Looking Glass and Chief Joseph came to them. Their faces betrayed little, though it was obvious their talks with the general council had not gone well.

"You may try to find out what you can, *Sinaskawin*," Joseph told her. "Go to Pen-del-ton if you wish."

"You don't sound too encouraging," Rebecca remarked candidly.

"I can't be. The council gives only seven suns. One of your weeks." Joseph sighed heavily and gazed at the ground. "After that, they say it will be war."

Chapter 11

A heavy, foglike mist swirled to treetop height along the Clearwater River. Rebecca Caldwell and Lone Wolf had awakened early and eaten a light breakfast in the longhouse. Now they went about their tasks for departure in the light of a shiny, yellow-white ball that rested on the eastern horizon. Its usual brilliance and rich orange morning color filtered out by the fall clouds, it provided wan and chilly illumination. *Hinmatoo Shanim* came to where they saddled horses.

"I would ride with you," he stated plainly.

"Not into the white man's village, surely," Rebecca responded.

"No. Only to a place where I might watch."

Lone Wolf yawned. The morning air invigorated him and gave freedom to his recovered memory. "Might be we could use a messenger. No telling what we'll find when we get there."

Fall Thunder smiled when Rebecca repeated the words in Lakota. *"Hinmahtooyahletkeht"* would send two of his warriors with us."

"That's all the better," Rebecca told him. "We can travel swiftly and safely along the trail left by the stolen horses."

"How will you get the white men to punish those who took them?" Fall Thunder inquired in a serious tone.

"That remains to be seen," Rebecca admitted a bit uncertainly.

"Never thought I'd admit it, but I miss that little fart," Clem Dye growled as he swung his bare, pale shanks out of the narrow bunk and probed underneath for his boots. "Gettin' up afore the sun to feed all them horses ain't my idea of life on the owl hoot trail."

A chuckle came from Sy Burton, who remained between his blankets. "You mean that now you admit there was some use for Thorne?"

"Yep. Now his lot falls to the rest of us. Say . . . how come you ain't got the dirty jobs to be doin'?"

Sy laughed softly once more. "Why, that sissy Englishman's taken a likin' to me. He asked me to be his bodyguard, startin' today. So I get out of all these farmhand chores."

"Don't laugh too loud, Sy. Talk I hear, he's gonna ride with us the next time out. He does an' you'll wind up playin' Step-An'-Fetch-It for him."

Sy threw a pillow at his friend as Clem darted through the door, three buttons of his shirt yet to be closed. A moment later, Clem poked his head around the corner of the half-open portal.

"See you at breakfast, Sy?"

"Sure thing. That new feller Bryce's got the right idea over at the Silver Dollar Cafe. Two for the price of one. Wonder where he got that from?"

"Hear he came over from Fort Missoula. Had him a' eatin' place there that went broke. Learned that trick from the guy who beat him out."

"All the better for us. Kiss them Appaloosies for me."

"Shee-it," Clem drawled as he departed.

A salt tang, miraculously transported from the far-off ocean, tinged the air of Pendleton, Oregon in the early morning damp. Far to the east a low ridge of hills blocked off the weak red rays of the low-riding fall sun. Winter couldn't be far away, Clem figured as he walked his horse along the sparsely populated main street toward the corrals, where the stolen horses neighed noisily for their morning ration of grain and hay.

Funny how they learn new ways so quickly, Clem speculated. Right near like folks. Habit. Like eatin' three squares a day, or always mounting from the left. Injuns did it from either side. Why not us? Clem reached a point some block from the corrals and saw a man and woman leaning on the top rail, looking at the hungry, restive animals. He gigged his mount and trotted up.

"Mornin'," he greeted levelly. "You folks lookin' to buy?"

"Might be," the man replied. "They're beautiful animals."

"That they are."

"Who owns them?" the woman inquired, nodding pointedly toward the sign above the door to the small office building. "Pendleton Livestock Company," it read.

"The boss is a feller named Styles. Roger Styles."

For a moment, Clem thought he saw a flicker of forge-hot anger in the pretty young woman's eyes. For a fact, they did widen and her jaw set slightly. He could have been mistaken, though, Clem considered at her next words.

"He must be new around here. I've not heard the name before."

"Only been here about four months or so. Came over from Dakota way after the Custer Massacre. I've been workin' for him since he started up. A good man."

"I'm sure he is."

Was it sarcasm he heard in her tone? Clem gave her a closer glance. And what a looker! Slim and straight, with what could be a hint of Indian in her blood, from the high cheekbones and slight cast to her lovely blue eyes and the long, black hair. Some traces of an early settler? Maybe the daughter of a mountain man and his Nez Percé squaw? Somehow, Clem had the feeling he had seen her somewhere before. The man beside her looked hard as horseshoes. He, too, appeared to have made a surprised reaction to Styles's name. Did they know the boss from somewhere else?

"What time does Mister Styles open the office?" The man interrupted Clem's reflections with the quiet question.

"Nine o'clock, usually. You can find him here by nine-thirty for sure."

"Thank you," the sweet-faced gal replied. Then she spoke to her companion. "Let's go find some breakfast and come back later, shall we?"

"Try the Silver Dollar, Miss," Clem volunteered. "Meals are two for the price of one and darn good grub, if you don't mind my sayin' so."

"Why, that's most kind of you. We'll look into that."

So saying, she and her companion turned away and walked down the main street. Grinning after them, Clem dismounted, tied off his mount, and strode bowlegged toward the twin stacks of hay.

Following the stolen horses to Pendleton had not been difficult. Over twelve hundred hoofs cut a wide swath in the virgin soil. The thieves had made no effort to cover

101

their tracks, and they had not encountered any dangers along the way. A suitable place had been located three miles from town where *Hinmatoo Sahnim* and the warriors from Chief Joseph's band made camp. Rebecca and Lone Wolf had changed into their "civilized" clothes and ridden on into Pendleton before sunup. The young woman and her stalwart companion had circled the town and then approached the livestock pens by way of a side street. They left their own mounts at the tie-rail in front of a funeral parlor and proceeded on foot. After their brief though irritatingly revealing conversation with Clem Dye they went directly to the cafe.

"Now what?" Lone Wolf inquired after the busy waitress brought them both steaming stoneware mugs of coffee.

"I might have known it. It's hard to believe that Roger would be this far from civilization. Yet, the whole scheme of stealing horses, even the ruthless murder of mere children, has all the marks of Roger's sort of crime. At least this time we have everything we need to see he doesn't get away with it."

"How's that?"

"The horses are here, in his corrals. He has posters up, advertising the sale of Palouse horses. His men are close at hand to be questioned, and we even have witnesses in the person of Fall Thunder and myself."

"It sounds a neat package, all right," Lone Wolf cautioned. "But let's not be too sure of that until we've talked with the local law."

"Which we shall do, promptly at eight o'clock this morning. Now, let's order breakfast and enjoy ourselves. I'm looking forward to finally finishing off Roger Styles before noon."

Sheriff Hezekiah Holman sat behind a smoothed and polished slab of native fir. The thick, rectangular slice had been lovingly finished by his loyal supporters, and a massive, matching chair mounted on a swivel base. Round, stout limbs, each larger than a big man's thighs, supported the ponderous chunk of wood and, if the sheriff suffered from a lack of drawer space, he gave no sign of it.

Neat stacks of "wanted" posters and other paperwork of his office sat squarely on each of the four corners of the top. A blotter, inkwell, and steel-nib pen occupied the center directly in front of him. Off to one side, a large cast-iron pot-bellied stove sat in readiness for winter's frigid blasts. A rack on the rough log wall held four Spencer repeating carbines and a pair of shotguns, one sawed off to some fifteen inches of barrel. An octagonal-cased pendulum clock sonorously ticked away the time, large brass hands pointing out the black Roman numerals on the white face. Behind the lawman, a yawning doorway bound in strap iron gave access to a cellblock containing four small cages made of fat steel bars. Sheriff Holman's pale gray eyes peered at his visitors over half-lens Franklin spectacles.

"Well now, what brings you folks here today? Those pesky danged Injuns been in yer chicken house again, have they?"

Not the best of men to solicit for their cause, Rebecca considered before answering. She took in the sheriff's spreading middle, his huge, work-roughed hands, and the bushy auburn hair that covered his round head like a forest. Thick liverish lips protruded in a wet pout. His breath wheezed in through a large, shovel-shaped nose and fluttered damply out from his mouth. The attempt he made at a smile had all the cordiality of a winter-starved timber wolf.

"Not chickens, Sheriff," Rebecca answered. "Horses. Nez Percé horses."

Holman cocked one bushy, gray-streaked eyebrow. "Oh? How's all that come about?"

"There is a man here in Pendleton. He is operating a large livestock company."

"Oh, sure. Everyone knows him," the sheriff interrupted. "That's Roger Styles. Fine man. Fine man indeed. What's he got to do with this?"

"He has nearly five hundred head of stolen horses in his corrals," Rebecca said levelly, fighting to keep calm in her voice.

"Now, I find that hard to believe, Miss. Uh, by the way, don't believe I got your names."

"Rebecca Caldwell. And this is Brett Baylor. We know Roger from the past. He's a dangerous criminal, and this time we have all we need to see he pays."

"Not if you're talkin' about Appaloosie horses, Miss Caldwell," the sheriff countered.

"What do you mean?" Rebecca demanded icily.

Holman gave her a patronizing twitch of a smile, addressing Rebecca as though speaking to a child. "Injuns ain't got any property rights. You should know that. If, as you claim, these horses at the Pendleton Company are Injun horses, why then there's no crime been committed."

"Somewhere I miss your logic, Sheriff. Oregon is a state, with duly constituted law enforcement. It is my understanding that theft is theft. There is nothing in any statute that says that a horse thief is exempt from the penalty if he steals an Indian's horse, any more than if he stole one belonging to, say, the sheriff of a county. Would you be so kind as to explain this strange quirk?"

"I just did. Them Nez Percés is off the reservation. Technically that makes 'em hostiles. Ain't no crime to steal from hostile Injuns."

Confounded, Rebecca attempted to refute the twisted reasoning of this bigoted lawman. "Let me enlighten you a little about Roger Styles. Roger Styles is wanted in seven states for cattle rustling, mayhem, murder, armed robbery, and half a dozen other offenses. There is also a federal warrant outstanding from the court in Fort Smith for his involvement in certain criminal activities in the Indian Territory.

"He comes here, he and his men steal hundreds of *Chopun-nish* horses, murder men and small boys, and you tell me he hasn't broken the law?"

"That's about the size of it, Miss Caldwell," Holman told her calmly, his thick fingers laced over his fat paunch.

"Since when has murder not been a crime?"

"We're talking about hostile Indians, Miss Caldwell, not 'civilized' ones who are living on their reservations, obeying the law."

"What the hell sort of law is that?"

Again the nasty, patronizing smile. "Good, solid, reasonable white man's law. I gather you're not from around here?"

"That's the first intelligent thing you've said since we came in here," Rebecca snapped.

"Now, now." Sheriff Holman raised a hand in

admonishment. "Mustn't get all testy about it. Let me explain a little to you. Since 'sixty-three, the military and civil administrators of the territory, and later the state, have been trying to get the Nez Percé on their reservation across the river in Idaho. I noticed you called them by that bastardized name they have for themselves, so I'd reckon you to be somehow related?"

"Wrong. I'm from Nebraska," Rebecca told him.

"However. To get on to what I wanted to say. The Injuns, at least most of them, refused. Old Chief Joseph was convinced to sign the treaty. Still, he didn't abide by it. Some eight or nine years ago, he died. His son took over the tribe. Except for a danged few of the heathen scum, the rest continue to offer resistance to the law of the United States. General Howard, the new military department commander, wants to make sure they are at last rounded up and put where they belong. He's opened a lot of land to white settlement. He's ordered all the bands to report to the reservation. So long as they do not, they are outside the law and as such, fair game to anyone who wants to take a crack at them. Thus, Roger and his men have not done anything wrong. Did that make everything clear enough for you?"

"For a simpleminded woman, do you mean, Sheriff?"

Holman nodded slightly before he realized her question had been a trap. Rebecca smiled sweetly and continued.

"That has no bearing. Roger Styles is a wanted man. Doesn't that have some importance to you?"

"Nope. So long as he's not wanted here. I think it would be wise, young lady, for you to forget bein' a champion of the noble red man and go back to Nebraska where some fine man—like Mr. Baylor here—can appreciate you and help you make a passel of kids. Leave the complicated 'Injun situation to those of us who understand it."

Red-faced, her anger spilling over in torrents, Rebecca came slowly to her feet. A quick movement by Lone Wolf prevented her from reaching into her fur and feather reticule. For a moment, she worked her mouth without sound coming, rendered inarticulate by her fury.

"That's . . . that's the most preposterous tissue of outright lies I've ever heard. You amaze me, Sheriff. Why is it that I somehow get the feeling you're on Roger Styles's payroll, rather than a public servant of the people of this county?"

Purpling, Holman sprang from his gigantic swivel chair and crashed one ham hand on his sturdy slab desk. "That's enough Miss Caldwell! Your accusations are reprehensible. Another unseemly outburst like that and I'll put you away in those cells back there."

"What if Mr. Baylor and I were to make the facts known to the public?"

"In that case, mere confinement in this jail would be the least of your worries. Do I make myself clear?"

"Oh, most definitely, Sheriff," Rebecca replied as she rose, gathered up her long tattersall dress hem, and walked toward the door. "And . . . thank you for your unstinting cooperation, Sheriff Holman."

Once outside, Rebecca exploded in a fashion more familiar to Lone Wolf. "Why that preposterous son of a bitch!"

"Take it easy, Becky. We're in a strange place. Let's find out how the wind blows. Take our time."

"Yes. We'll have to go slow." A crusading light glowed in Rebecca's deep blue eyes. "But not for long."

Chapter 12

"It ain't right, I tell ya," a grizzled old man at the bar in the Pendleton hotel declared vehemently. He slammed the heavy glass foot of his beer schooner down for emphasis.

Rebecca Caldwell and Lone Wolf sat at a table to one side, beyond the open trellis of wooden bars that separated the common saloon from the "Ladies' Bar." The old-timer's outburst shattered the atmosphere of quiet and attracted their attention.

"What ain't right, Salty?" a beefy man halfway down the bar inquired.

"Cagin' up them Appaloosie horses. They ain't wild critters. They belong to someone. That makes it horse stealin' in my book. An' you know what's done to horse thieves."

"*Who* do they belong to, Salty?" his inquisitor pressed.

"Why to the Nez Percé, that's who."

"Oh. Just a batch of Injuns."

"Just a batch of Injuns. Just a batch of Injuns," Salty mimicked. "Lissen here. The law's the law. Stealin' horses is again' the law."

The thick-shouldered, red-faced man stepped closer and spoke softly, his tone kindly as he gave his advice. "Best be careful where you say things like that, Salty. I've got no beef with the Nez Percé. They're sittin' on land I'd like to add to my spread. All the same, I've got to agree with you in part."

"What do you mean by being careful *where* I say things, Howard?"

Howard Barnes looked at Salty levelly. "Like over at the bank. Or maybe around the Sheriff's office. Or even here . . . when that English feller is around. Those three have been mighty chummy of late with this Mr. Roger Styles."

Rebecca signaled to the bartender. He came from behind the mahogany and stopped at their table.

"Those gentlemen there, would you ask them to join us, please?" the lovely young woman requested of him.

"Right away, Miss."

"I'm Howard Barnes," the large man effused as he came to the table. "An' this here is Old Salty."

"Clement Salters," the old-timer offered.

"Gentlemen, I'm Rebecca Caldwell and this is my friend, Brett Baylor. We overheard your sentiments a moment ago and we have to agree. We are rather well acquainted with Roger Styles and, to put it mildly, he is a crook. A master schemer who has evaded justice entirely too long."

"How long might that be, Miss Caldwell?" Salty inquired.

"More than ten years, if members of what used to be his gang can be believed. He has subverted lawmen before. For some mysterious reason, bankers tend to fawn over him. Madams do his bidding for nothing more

109

than a smile."

"Yeah," Howard said wonderingly. "Him and Miss Jane had been mighty tight of late. I wondered why. He seems such a, ah, dandy."

"If we were to describe Roger's habits in that department, it would gag you," Lone Wolf added.

Barnes scowled. "Why would he be in a risky business like selling horses if he's an outlaw?"

"Everything Roger does has a veil of legitimacy about it. As to dealing in horses, since he apparently gets his stock in trade free, it cuts down on overhead and increases profits. That's what Roger's best at. He did a similar thing with cattle down in Kansas."

Mention of Roger's rustling scheme brought images to Rebecca's mind of Bobby Rhodes. For a moment her pulse raced as she envisioned his smooth, sun-browned skin, his small but able manhood, so lusty and satisfying. She saw, too, his wonder and delight at discovering the secrets of love. Oh, how well they had fitted together. Her loins tingled with the memory. Suddenly she realized that Lone Wolf had been speaking.

". . . the Sheriff. What connection does he have?"

"I mentioned him because he's been quite friendly to Styles over the past few weeks. Could be he's tryin' to promote himself a free Appaloosie, or a big contribution for his campaign. Election coming up next year."

"Or he might be in this horse stealing with Roger?" Rebecca asked.

"Hummm. Couldn't rightly say," Howard admitted. "Hez Holman's not been mixed into anything dishonest before, far's anyone around here knows."

"He certainly gave us a runaround," Rebecca remarked. "Even defined the law as it not being a crime

110

to steal from the Nez Percé. He's either an Indian hater or he's in it with Roger."

"Oh, he's got no love for redskins, sure enough. He lost a wife and a young'n' to the Cheyenne comin' out to these parts in sixty-seven. He's remarried since an' it's no happy little home he's got. T'way some folks' got it, him an' his wife sort of survive on mutual hate."

"Why, Salty, you're a regular gossip, aren't you?" Rebecca teased.

Clement Salters blushed and offered a weak grin. "Comes with old age, I suppose."

"I was only having a bit of fun," Rebecca explained. Then she summed up their meager supply of new information. "Well, it looks as though we'll have to wait and see about the Sheriff. Something should be done about those horses, though."

"Could be somethin' might get done, if some folks put a mind to it." Salty gave Rebecca a broad, knowing wink.

Silhouetted against the frosty dome of stars, a silent figure detached itself from the darkness between buildings and hurried to the rear door of the Pendleton Livestock Company. A brief rap of knuckles was answered within seconds and the visitor entered quickly.

"Well, to what occasion do I owe this nocturnal visit, Sheriff?" Roger Styles inquired jovially. He crossed to the sideboard and poured stiff shots of brandy into two crystal balloon glasses. He offered one to the lawman and seated himself at his rolltop desk.

"We've got some trouble, Roger."

"Hezekiah, you amaze me. When does a struggling new business not have trouble?"

"True. But this is the sort that can't be laughed away or solved with money." Holman paused a moment, preparing the words before he spoke them. "There's a woman in town. Says she's known you for some time and that you're a wanted man in several states."

"True enough. You knew that when we began our little, ah, partnership." Roger remained glib enough, yet deep within lurked an icy suspicion he knew of only one woman who would say such a thing. "Go on."

"She says that those horses out there are stolen and that your men killed some Injun kids in the takin' of em'."

"You knew from the start that we got the horses from the Nez Percé. Thing is, they didn't want to give them up easily. So a little blood got spilled. That's nothing a bit of that money you were talking about won't cure."

"Don't get me wrong. I'm not askin' for a bigger cut, Roger. I'm worried. If she took this to the state people in Salem, we could be in a lot of trouble."

"The boys aren't taking any horses from Oregon. We're only selling them here. That's legal. You said so yourself."

"I'm not a lawyer. I could be wrong. It's the same thing, though, if they go to the Army. General Howard is responsible for policing Idaho territory."

"Dammit, Hezekiah, I went ahead on your assurances . . ." Roger began to bluster.

"I said, so long as no one complained—and no one around here would—there wouldn't be any trouble. Now this outsider comes here and lays all this out to me."

"This woman, what's her name?"

"Caldwell. Reb . . ."

"Rebecca Caldwell!" Roger exploded as the color

112

drained from his face. "Goddammit, how did she find me here?"

"Y-you know her then?"

"Oh, yes. I know her only too well. She . . . she . . ." Roger drew another breath. In a state of near-apoplexy, he had to struggle to regain control. "She's all but ruined me. Not once, but more than half a dozen times."

"She said you ran a gang of hard cases through a man named Jake Tulley."

"So what if I did? Jake's dead, so are most of his boys. That bitch, Rebecca, has it in her head that I'm responsible for her and her mother being traded off to the Sioux by Tulley. I had nothing to do with it. Even so, she's meddled in my affairs over the past two years to the extent that I arrived here nearly broke. The time has come to put an end to her and her troublemaking. You said she was in town. Is she still here?"

"Yes. Over at the hotel."

"Then I think you and I had better go over there and finish this thing."

"You mean arrest her on some trumped up charge?"

"I mean kill her."

"There's no way I can stand by and ignore a murder."

"What do you think I'm paying you for? You won't just stand by, you'll pull the trigger. Now, let's go."

Three persons crouched beside the big gate to the corrals behind Roger Styles's livestock company office. The moon had not yet risen, and they had waited quietly in the darkness until they saw Roger and the Sheriff leave and walk away down the main street.

"The inner gates should be opened first," Rebecca

113

suggested. "Then all we have to do is run them out through here." —

"Right good idea, Missy," Salty agreed.

Swiftly the trio went to work. They had opened only three of the inner gates when a shot, followed by a roar of anger, came from the direction of the hotel.

"She's not here! Dammit, where did she go?"

A moment of silence came in which Rebecca, Lone Wolf, and Old Salty raced toward the front gate. At least, Rebecca reconciled herself, some of the Appaloosies would be free.

"The horses! Goddammit! She's going after the horses." Still inside the hotel, the terrible revelation came to Roger as he bolted down the stairs.

"Hurry!" Rebecca shouted as she reached the outer gate.

With all three shoving, the heavy wooden pole frame swung outward into the street. As one, the three rescuers rushed for the farthest open pen. There they began to shout and wave their arms.

Slowly at first, then in a whinnying, stomping stream, the Nez Percé horses streaked from the corral and down the wide main street.

"There they go! Stop 'em! Stop 'em!" Roger Styles shouted from a block and a half away. "Oh, that rotten bitch!"

Every second grew more precious. Knowing that, Rebecca still took time to stop and carefully aim at Roger's portly frame. She squeezed off a round that cracked past under Roger's left armpit, punching through the back of his coat. He howled in alarm and leaped to the side of the street. From under his coat, he drew a short-barreled .45 Colt. Wild-eyed he sought only to avenge himself on Rebecca Caldwell.

Before he could, a hundred spotted-rump ponies thundered past in a billow of dust. When the last of them went by, Roger could see nothing of Rebecca.

They found Fall Thunder and the two Wallowa warriors where they had made camp along a small creek. Rebecca dismounted and walked to *Hinmahtoo Sahnim*.

"We couldn't get them all. Not enough time. We did free some of the horses. You'll have to round them up and take them back. Tell Chief Joseph that Roger Styles is the man responsible. He's alerted now. That will make it more difficult for us to get the others out of the corrals."

"What did lawman do?"

Rebecca made a wry face. "Unfortunately, *Wahlitits* was right about this particular white man. He's apparently involved with Roger in stealing the horses. After we talked to him, he went to warn Roger. The way he'll see it, what we did will be called a crime. So now we have to avoid arrest and try to free the horses. Tell Chief Joseph we need more time. A week won't be enough."

"*Wahlitits* and many of the young men will be angry. We will do as you ask, but maybe they won't wait. Maybe they come here to kill this man Roger and the lawman."

"Oh, no. No, Fall Thunder. That would be the worst thing they could do. Get us enough time to do it my way. Please. Your people will suffer greatly if you do not."

"We go now, to find the horses and take them back. I will talk to *Himahtooyahletkeht*. I'm afraid you won't have any more time. The old men talk, the young ones want to fight. Maybe there is nothing we can do."

"For all our sakes, I hope you're wrong," Rebecca replied sincerely.

Chapter 13

Two posses had been sent out in as many days. Rebecca and Lone Wolf kept busy dodging them and working on some reliable plan to release the ponies and kill Roger Styles. They rode quietly along a narrow path through the thick forest of fir and pine. Jays quarreled above in the branches and squirrels scolded them for breaking the peaceful quiet of the virgin timber. A soft pounding on the thickly mulched ground came from behind them and halted their progress.

"Another posse?" Rebecca asked in a hushed voice.

"No. Only one horse."

"A messenger from Chief Joseph!" Rebecca declared expectantly.

"We'll have to wait and see."

"Then we'd better get off into the trees and see who it is before announcing ourselves."

Lone Wolf grinned. "Good idea."

They dismounted and led their horses in among the tightly spaced trunks of mossy-barked behemoths. The tangy-sweet scent of pine resin permeated the air. Tensely they waited.

The lone figure appeared at last, silhouetted against

the morning light. He rode a short distance beyond where they had left the trail, then reined in and turned back. In the time it took, Rebecca had recognized him.

"It's Fall Thunder."

Lone Wolf nodded and they rode out into view.

"I was careless," Fall Thunder wryly noted.

"You were in a hurry," Rebecca amended for him. "Do you bring news from the council?"

Fall Thunder's brow furrowed and he nodded curtly. "Not good news. *Wahlitits* and his faction have won over more on the council. They will not wait beyond the seven days agreed to. This time, nothing Looking Glass said would change their minds."

"What about Joseph?"

"He had left for Wallowa. Looking Glass and White Goose stood alone against the council. *Wahlitits* argued that seven tens of horses were not enough to keep the whites from their deserved punishment. It's . . . not much time," Fall Thunder ended weakly.

"It's what time we have," Rebecca acknowledged with a shrug. "Go back to the council. Tell them we are going to Idaho. We'll attack the men who are stealing the horses. If *Wahlitits* and the young men want to do something useful, tell them to join us. It's wrong to war against innocent settlers. If we can make it hot enough for Roger's men, they'll quit him. Then we can work to get back the horses already stolen."

Fall Thunder considered that for a moment. "That's wise. I will speak for it before the council. Others will, too. Where will we meet?"

"If the warriors don't come before the time is up, look for us on the big bend of the Snake River."

Again Fall Thunder nodded. "That's good." Then he

117

gave her the warrior's salutation. "Fight bravely."

Touched by his gravity and the honor, Rebecca reached out and laid a hand on his bronze arm. "I'll save a few for you if I can."

"I will be there." Then Fall Thunder studied the sky, studded with tiny puffy clouds. "It's going to snow."

"No," Rebecca responded, unconvinced. "Why, it's a beautiful day."

"Tomorrow, next day, snow. I can smell it in the air."

"Let's hope it doesn't snow in Idaho."

"Bloody hell!" Clive Reversford exploded when an unnoticed branch slapped his face. "Fine time to be chasing around out here in the wilderness. I thought we'd be sticking close to town to guard the horses from that woman."

"'That woman,' as you put it," Roger Styles informed him, "would expect us to do just that. So we go after replacements for the ones she let loose. It's a simple exercise in logic."

"It might be simple to you, but I don't find breaking one's arse on one of these abominable American saddles to be such a brilliant strategy."

"At least you came along this time." Roger mellowed slightly. "The men appreciate that and so do I. I particularly like those tins of fancy foods you provided for us."

"One needn't be a barbarian," Clive answered fussily. "Ah, Roger, there's something I heard this morning that I wanted to mention. Some of our local badmen are saying it's going to snow. Could that be possible?"

Roger gazed around him at the golden shafts of

sunlight that pierced the tall evergreens. "I doubt it. It's warm, sunny, only a few clouds. By tomorrow, we'll be in Idaho and headed back with more Appaloosies before nightfall. Relax and enjoy the ride, Clive."

Rebecca and Lone Wolf made camp to the east of Wallowa Valley. The next day would put them into Idaho. Throughout the afternoon, they had encountered the sign of many horses. While their evening meal cooked over a small, low fire, Rebecca pondered the meaning of this.

"Shod hoofs . . . and so many. Lone Wolf, it has to be Roger's gang. We're only a few miles behind them. He surely left some men in Pendleton to watch the corrals. That improves our odds in attacking those ahead of us."

"I count easily more than a dozen. They're riding so close together that it's not possible to be more accurate. There could be as many as twenty. That's not the best of odds."

"We're not going to face them in a head-to-head gunfight. We can lay ambushes, take a few shots at them, and slip away. That way we're constantly after them. At least until *Wahlitits* and his warriors get here."

"You're that sure they'll come?"

"*Wahlitits* is frantic to get the fighting started. He's not likely to turn down the only game in town."

By noon the next day, Rebecca and Lone Wolf had ridden beyond the gang and set up their first ambush. Rebecca felt certain she knew the rustler's destination. Their course had swung nearly due north, toward *Peopeo Kiskiak Hihi's* scattered villages in Tepahlewan Canyon on the Salmon River. The closeness of this location

119

offered few chances to harass the outlaws, though Rebecca determined to make the most of what time they had. Sheltered by the fat trunks of huge pines, she and Lone Wolf waited on opposite sides of the trail, tensing at the distant drumming of hoof beats.

At a brisk, steady pace, the gang drew nearer. Rebecca held her light Winchester saddle carbine at the ready, sighting along the barrel to the point where she expected to see the first riders. They came into view two minutes later.

Rebecca didn't recognize the tall, lanky man in the lead. A careless lock of wavy blond hair flopped on his forehead, and a light sheen of perspiration dampened his long, horsey face. Unconsciously, she held her breath while the first three men rode by. Odd. She had made a quick count and there appeared to be less rustlers than had been expected. Only ten men. The last of these came closer as she took up slack on the trigger.

Three fast rounds levered through Rebecca's Winchester. One rider flung his arms wide and spun sideways in the saddle, before pitching onto the spongy bed of the forest. A second outlaw cried out and clutched at his chest. The heavy boom of Lone Wolf's Spencer sounded, and a third hard case fell dead. Then Rebecca ran to her horse.

She swung into the saddle and heeled her mount in the ribs. In seconds she had faded away into the anonymity of the trees. On the far side, she knew, Lone Wolf did the same.

"Gad! Someone's shooting at us!" Clive Reversford exclaimed from the head of the small column.

"Get your head down and let's get outta here," Clem Dye advised.

"We're just going to leave the others behind?"

"Unless you want to die and lose yer hair in the bargain."

"You've got a point, my good man," Clive readily agreed, putting spurs to his mount.

Roger had divided the gang early in the morning, going on with the other group to scout out the Nez Percé villages and locate the herd. Clive Reversford had continued on with this contingent. The men might make fun of his elaborate tent and costly tins of special food, but they had grown friendly in a rough sort of way. Enough so that until the shots had come out of nowhere, he had been enjoying the trip. The ambush put a new value on things. Particularly his continued good health. From behind he heard the noisy pounding of many hoofs.

A quick glance showed him the survivors of the gang riding furiously to catch up. Would whoever shot at them follow? The question nagged at him until Clem signaled for a walk and the mad gallop ceased.

"We've outrun 'em by now," Clem assured him.

"Who were they?"

"Don't know. Injuns most likely. But . . . they *was* usin' rifles."

"Could it be that Caldwell woman?"

"No tellin'. Whatever the case, I hope that's the last we see of 'em."

"My sentiments exactly, old boy," Clive expounded fervently.

By noon the next day, Rebecca and Lone Wolf had struck twice more, killing two men and wounding three others. Weather conditions had worsened suddenly, though. The temperature dropped a good thirty degrees and a biting cold wind drove down out of the northwest. Thick, dark clouds covered the heavens. Made nervous by the sudden change, the horses twitched their ears and rippled their shiny coats. Rebecca patted her roan's neck and spoke soothingly.

"Fall Thunder and his damned snow," Lone Wolf groused. "He might have called it right after all."

"It'll put Roger's men to a standstill, if it comes. That we could use to advantage."

"We'll soon get to know about that," Lone Wolf remarked as the first flurries of delicate white flakes tumbled out of the sky.

When it came in earnest, thick clouds of snow whipped along by moaning, slashing wind turned the world into a blinding monochrome. Rebecca could not speak nor hear over the tumult. She quickly lost sight of Lone Wolf and he of her.

Rapidly the temperature plummeted far below the freezing mark. Wet, heavy flakes plastered against the north and west exposures of trees and bushes. Rebecca wandered aimlessly in a swirling alabaster world. Here and there sharp reports, ever so like gunshots, sounded as branches burst under the tremendous load of the untimely blizzard.

"Lone Wolf!" she yelled into the arctic blast. "Lone Wolf!"

No response came. Rebecca drew and fired one of her Smith Americans. The triple report seemed absorbed in the deadening effect of the storm. Again she called out.

"Lone Wolf!" It was like shouting into a pillow.

"I . . . mmm . . . ver . . . he . . ."

For a moment Rebecca thought she heard his voice,

faintly and at great distance. She fired the remaining two shots.

Nothing.

She trembled with cold, although bundled in all the warm clothing she possessed. Her cheeks and nose felt stiff and brittle and her eyes watered constantly. A blizzard in October. Unusual even for here. All the same it came.

The world turned solid white.

Chapter 14

Night came in the howling tumult, with only a slightly perceptible change in illumination. Rebecca had wrapped her feet and legs in every piece of cloth in her saddle bags. Bundled in her heavy coat, a blanket over that and a rain slicker atop it, she still shook violently from the cold. Numbness began to set in and each breath was filled with needles of icy pain. She began to fear that either she or her horse would surrender to the blizzard and slip quietly into death.

"No!" she shouted vehemently into the teeth of the storm.

Rebecca slapped her thighs in an effort to stimulate circulation. Then she flopped her arms like a chicken trying its wings. Spooked by the tempest, and her antics, the roan gelding whickered nervously. A moment later a sudden lurch by her mount shot new awareness through Rebecca's body. For a while, at least, she would remain alert.

While she did, Rebecca sought to gain her bearings. Instinctively her roan had turned tail to the storm. That put her in roughly a southeasterly direction. More east than south, she judged. If only she could find some shelter, build a fire. Thoughts of warmth only rekindled her despair.

Would this be where she would die? Alone, not to be found until the unprecedented early blizzard released its frigid grasp on the earth? At a laggard pace, the gelding bore her over the ground.

Unnoticed at first, awareness began to seep away, along with physical sensation. Slowly, the confining walls of swirling whiteness faded out. Rebecca's head drooped.

Four men huddled around the small camp stove in Clive Reversford's tent. The iron bucket of coals gave out little warmth, though enough to prevent them from freezing. In another part of Sibley, the remainder of Clive's men took shelter from the blizzard.

"Bloody snow in October. Who would ever have believed it!" Reversford declared for the twentieth time. "Clem, do you imagine Roger and the others managed to round up any horses before this storm descended on them?"

"Can't be sure. All I want now is to get warm."

"Put more charcoal on the grate and we can fix some coffee and tinned beef. That can warm us from the inside as well."

"You know, Clive, I thought haulin' meat around in cans was the craziest thing I ever came across. Only now . . . seems you sure planned well for any problems." Clive dropped three large chunks of kiln-charred oak into the brazier.

Clive flushed slightly at this sincere compliment from a ruffian like Clem Dye. Pleased, he answered modestly.

"I can certainly say I hadn't a blizzard in mind when I made provision for this food. As things stand, we can wait out the storm and be quite cozy all the while. Well fed, I might add."

"We're grateful. No way we could find game in all this."

Clive dug into another gunnysack and pulled out two round, flat cans of boiled beef. He rummaged around in a small box and found an onion and some dry red peppers. He began opening one tin with his belt knife.

"There's some potatoes in that other bag. We can make a stew of it, what?"

"Sure hope the boss an' them boys found some shelter," Clem said sincerely while he sorted through the supplies for the potatoes.

"If they didn't, it looks like you and I are running this enterprise," Clive observed.

A strange expression washed over Clem's face. "By golly, you're right. I never thought of it that way."

"One must always hold to the main course."

"An' ours is to make money off these horses."

"By Jove, you've the makings of a first class rogue, Clem."

"Uh . . . thanks, I guess."

Reversford cocked his head. "The wind seems to be abating slightly. Perhaps we're going to be fortunate."

"None too soon. Anyone caught out there's froze to a block of ice by now."

She woke up with a violent snap of her head. Utter silence had aroused her.

Low clouds still obscured Rebecca's view, yet the

126

raging winds had slackened and her world of darkness seemed to hold its breath in anticipation of what might come next. How far had her horse wandered while she slept? Rebecca felt nothing now, not even the hot sensation of frostbite on her muffled face. Frothy icicles hung from her gelding's muzzle. Its labored breath came in clouds of white. The animal had nearly reached its limit. So had she, Rebecca realized with sinking spirit. They had to find somewhere to shelter, and soon. Nothing else mattered.

"Keep going, old boy," she urged in a croaking voice.

The deep snow creaked and groaned under the animal's unsteady tread. A slight breeze high in the treetops sent cascades of powdery crystals falling about her, while the boughs loudly protested their burden. Still Rebecca could not see the stars. Minutes creeped across this all-but-silent land, and she thought to call for Lone Wolf again.

Three shots, which seemed to be swallowed by the overwhelming quiet, barked from one of her Smith .44's. "Lone Wolf! Lone Wolf! Can you hear me?"

Tensely, Rebecca waited. No longed-for hail came to her.

Grimly, she rode on.

She had no idea how long she had been guiding her mount toward it, or even when she had first seen it. A small pinpoint of yellow lay close to the horizon. In this vast wilderness of snow and darkness, no estimate of its size or distance could be made. It might be a mile away or two hundred yards. There! It flickered. Not the sun, she acknowledged. Rebecca begged her roan to hold on a bit longer.

When the animal floundered a few minutes later,

Rebecca slid painfully from the saddle. She stumbled to the roan's muzzle and gently chafed away the accumulation of ice and snow. Then she took the reins in her left hand and started out, staggering toward the unknown amber beacon that tauntingly seemed not to grow in size, rather to remain the same and constantly recede into the distance.

"Oh, it has to be fixed," she said aloud, like part of a litany. "It has to be a farm or a village. Oh, let it be."

Did her eyes trick her? Or had the mysterious glow ceased to elude her? It appeared to grow larger now. A warm, welcoming brightness in the hellish misery of the night. Only a bit farther now. A hundred paces . . . seventy . . . She could make out the darker outline of a low, squarish cabin, the light—it had to be a kerosene lamp—shining from an oiled paper window. Rebecca took heart and floundered through the waist-high snow. She grunted and panted as she dragged her horse along. Thirty paces to go . . .

"Hello in the house!" she managed to call out before she pitched face first into the snow.

"Let's get these things off of you so you can be warmed by the fire."

The pleasing features of a handsome, square-faced young man hovered fuzzily above Rebecca. She blinked and tried to focus her eyes. Her mind struggled to sort meaning out of his words. Her rain slicker crackled with splintering ice as he deftly removed it with thick, blunt fingers. The muffler had been removed from Rebecca's face, and she felt a tingling sensation as warm air caressed her numbed flesh.

128

"There now. The blanket next," urged the soft, baritone voice.

Rebecca moved feebly in an effort to cooperate. She knew now that he wanted to take off her clothes. What a strange time to be doing that, an errant thought stabbed. Odder still, the idea excited her.

With her erotic rush, blood flowed rapidly to her face and brought with it pain. She gasped and raised a hand to touch her frigid cheek.

"It's not frost bitten," the stranger assured her. "Here now, let's do for that coat."

When it came away, he saw her bead-decorated elkhide dress. "Are you all right?" he inquired in Shahaptian.

"I am Dakota, and do not speak the *Cho-pun-nish* tongue," Rebecca managed in rusty English.

"Wha? . . . What is a Sioux doing out here?"

"I came to buy Palouse horses."

"You speak excellent English."

"My mother was white."

"Oh . . . I see. Uh . . . do you want me to leave while you get out of that dress?"

"No need, really. I lived with the Oglala for five years. One thing I didn't acquire was a white woman's sense of false modesty. If it won't bother you, it won't me." Rebecca reached as if to remove her dress, groaned, and looked at the squatting man with appeal. "It looks like you're going to have to do it for me anyhow."

"Um . . . er, ah . . . yes."

Although he glanced away at first, her lovely body compelled him to look back more than once. Each time, his eyes lingered longer. With the dress off, he took a warming blanket from the hearth and wrapped her nakedness in it. Then he lifted and carried her to a place beside the fire.

"I'm, ah, Thad Walsh. This is my homestead. I live here with my son, Jamie, and daughter, Elizabeth."

"I'm Rebecca Caldwell. I . . . ah . . ."

"My wife died nearly a year ago. She was a Nez Percé."

"I'm sorry. A man needs his woman at his side. And the children. They must miss her terribly."

"They do. I certainly do. Let me get you some coffee."

"Oh, thank you so much, Thad."

The scalding liquid soon revived Rebecca. She breathed deeply and made light conversation with Thad Walsh. Then her eyelids began to flicker and slide downward. She yawned, stretched catlike, and drifted off into a deep sleep.

Diffused light from heavy cloud cover flooded the room when Rebecca at last awakened. Black shoe-button eyes peered downward at her from the cherubic face of an Indian boy. Above his high cheekbones and bronze skin, a mop of yellow hair, like an unruly halo, crowned the child's head.

"I'm Jamie," the boy announced. "What's your name?"

"Rebecca," came the answer. "I'm glad to meet you, Jamie. Where's your father? What time is it? Is anyone else here?" The questions came in a rapid flow as memory rushed back to her consciousness.

"Ask me slower. I can't remember more'n one at a time."

Rebecca smiled weakly at the lad and levered herself into an upright position. "All right, Jamie. Where's your father?"

"He's out gettin' wood for the fire. Can you speak Shahaptian?"

"No. I don't."

Jamie wrinkled his brow. "Too bad. I speak it better than this."

"Too bad you don't speak Lakota. I speak it better than this," Rebecca teased. "Now, what time is it? And what day?"

Jamie's lips formed a thoughtful pucker. "I can't tell time yet. And it's the day after the storm. Lots of snow on the ground."

An involuntary shudder trembled through Rebecca's body at mention of the blizzard. "How many days did it snow?"

"Two. The storm came one day, right before supper. It lasted most all of the night. Then it snowed for two more days."

"My goodness. It must be very high."

"Oh, it is. But Poppa says the sun will be out by tomorrow or the next day, and it will all melt away."

"I certainly hope so," Rebecca replied absently.

"Oh, I don't. It's fun to play in the snow. And to track rabbits. Why don't you like the snow, Rebecca?"

"I nearly died in that storm. Give me a chance to get over that, will you?"

Jamie giggled. "Poppa said to tell you there is hot soup and some cornbread."

"Just what I need!" Rebecca enthused. Unthinking, she started to rise, then quickly covered herself with the blanket. Jamie's eyes were round and his mouth formed a silent "oh."

"You sure are pretty, Rebecca."

"Thank you, Jamie. You're a bit young to be noticing that, aren't you?"

"I'm nearly five."

"All the same, I need to get dressed. Maybe your father wouldn't want you here while I do."

"He wouldn't mind, an' neither would I. Would it make you feel better if I took off my clothes, too?"

"Uh . . . er, no, not really, Jamie."

Still covered by the blanket, Rebecca came to her feet, swayed slightly, then grew steady. She stepped down onto the huge bearskin that lay before the fireplace and turned her back on the boy. Quickly she dropped the woolen cover and donned her elkhide dress. Rebecca slipped dainty feet into her beaded Sioux moccasins and turned back toward the room.

Jamie still stared with rapt concentration. His eyes shined brightly and he quickly wiped away a bemused smile. He'd never seen a real woman's bottom before. Only his little sister's, and that didn't count. The door banged open and Thad Walsh stepped in with a high-piled armload of firewood.

"Ah. You're back among the living, I see. Good. Did Jamie tell you there is soup and bread? Let me put this down and I'll get you a mug of coffee."

"I . . . I'm starving. Was I really out for more than two days?"

"That you were." Thad dumped the wood in a rick by the fireplace. "Jamie, get our guest a chair."

"Yes, Poppa." Jamie crossed to one wall and hefted a handmade chair. As he brought it to the table, he winked at Rebecca.

"Jamie's a sweet boy. He was keeping watch on me when I awakened."

Thad grinned with pride. "It's hard. Trying to be mother and father to him and his sister."

"You seem to have done well enough."

132

"Not actually. I . . . miss my wife terribly. I'm thinking of the years to come. There's just some things a father can't . . . er, do for a daughter."

While he spoke, Thad ladled a thick broth into a large wooden bowl and set it before Rebecca. He took a round slab of cornbread from the warmer over the cooking surface and put it out with a crock of butter and a knife.

"We have some dried camas bulbs stored in the root cellar. They're good dipped in honey. Jamie, why don't you go down and get some?"

"Sure, Poppa."

Jamie disappeared through a small trapdoor in one corner of the large main room. Rebecca started in on the savory soup. Her stomach cramped with emptiness as she breathed in the rich aroma.

"How soon can I be traveling?"

"Is there so much rush, then?"

"I don't mean it that way. I have a friend out there somewhere. We were separated in the storm. I'm anxious for his survival."

"His?" Thad asked a bit cooly.

"He—Lone Wolf—has been a partner of mine for a long while." Rebecca went on to explain her relationship to Lone Wolf and her quest to get vengeance. Thad stared at her, eyes round with wonder. When her tale ended, she concluded with a simple comment.

"And, of course, I don't want to put you out at all."

Impulsively, drawn by the wan beauty of the half-Sioux girl and her story of dangerous adventure, Thad reached out and placed a hand over one of hers. "You're not putting me out at all. On the contrary, I'm happy for your company. It'll be at least a day or two before the trails are clear. You are more than welcome to stay here with us until then."

Vagrant stirrings warmed Rebecca's loins as she looked deeply into Thad's green eyes. A shock of his flaxen hair fell across his brow, and this only quickened Rebecca's consciousness of him as a man. Her pulse increased and it took effort to draw her studied concentration away from his broad shoulders and generous mouth. Rebecca cleared her throat before she could trust herself to speak.

"Well, then, if I'm to be an unpaying guest for a while, I ought to do something to earn my keep. What do you need doing that requires a woman's touch?"

"No. I won't hear of that. You nearly died out in that blizzard. What you need is rest, warmth, good food, and some tender care."

"Tender, *loving* care?" An imp in Rebecca's mind forced the bold question out. Its raw presence between them caused her to blush.

"Er, ah, that's, er, not exactly . . . what . . ."

"I'm sorry. I've embarrassed you. But I mean it. I want to do what I can. I'm perfectly able to clean house, mend clothes, tell stories to the children at bedtime. Anything you need."

"You've been married yourself?"

"Yes. And widowed . . . twice before I turned eighteen. *Absa* warriors raided the Oglala village I lived in. Killed my husband and son in one attack, killed my second man another time. I . . . never really got to be much of a mother. So . . . it would please me greatly to 'make do' for you three while the snows melt."

"On that condition, we gladly accept. Jamie will be pleased and Elizabeth needs some mothering."

"About what, Poppa?" Jamie inquired as he climbed

from the cellar.

"Rebecca is going to stay with us until the snow goes away. She wants to do some things for you and Elizabeth. We both think you need a little mothering."

"Oh, that's larapin' good!" Jamie cried, jumping up and down. Then you can tell us stories and fix my britches and Lizbet's drawers," he enthused, and added slyly, "Will you be sleepin' in Poppa's bed?"

"Jamie!" his father blurted, embarrassment coloring his face like a sunset.

Rebecca and Thad exchanged startled looks at this outburst. The hot glow in their eyes declared a different emotion. They seemed to say, in mutual silence. "Yes. Why not? If you'll have me."

"I'm sorry. Here's the camas bulbs. They don't even smell musty."

". . . and so, the Moon Princess punished Coyote by putting him into the body of a four-legs, so he could not fly through the night any more and do mischief. And that's why Coyote howls at the moon when it is full," Rebecca concluded to two drowsy, tossled heads. "Good night, Elizabeth. Good night, Jamie."

"G'night, Rebecca," Jamie replied dreamily. "I love stories about Coyote. Tell us another, please?"

"Tomorrow night."

"Promise?"

"I do."

"G'night."

Rebecca climbed from the loft and took a place on the hearth, at Thad's side, while he rocked slowly in a handcrafted rocker and sucked at his pipe. Thad reached down and gently placed a hand on her raven tresses.

"You know, I'd forgotten how important stories were to children."

"Most men do. That's why nearly all the Indian tribes have storytellers as an important part of every village society." Rebecca moved closer and laid her cheek against the strong pillar of his left thigh.

"Are you . . . sure they're both asleep?" Thad's voice came out a croak.

"Yes. Soundly. If I stay here much longer, I'm going to run out of Sioux children's stories."

"I'd like that."

"For me to run out?"

"For you to stay that long. I . . . ." Thad slid from the rocking chair to the hearth and impetuously embraced Rebecca. "I miss my wife for more than . . . than the sake of a well-kept home and someone to mother my children. I'm lonely, Rebecca. Frightfully so."

"Thad . . . Thad, I'm here, now, I won't disappear like smoke. Hold me and let your unhappiness go."

A moan of grief and wretchedness escaped Thad as he clung to Rebecca. They rocked back and forth a while, until his tensions eased. Then tautness of another nature infected them both. Thad's hand found a pert, firm breast and cupped it.

He squeezed gently, then with increased strength as Rebecca let her head sink back, lips parted and eyes slit in passion. Her hand groped in his lap and discovered the hardness there.

"Do you . . . will you . . . I mean . . ."

"Oh, yes, Thad. Yes. I want you more than anything in the world right now. Hurry. Come to me."

Clothing flew in several directions. Rebecca raged inwardly with a fire of erotic delight. Her loins tingled as Thad began to touch her.

Quickly she reached for his protruding maleness and stroked it as desire mounted. Choking sobs of long-suppressed ardor burst from Thad's lips and, in a frenzy of delirious abandon, he buried his face between her outstretched thighs.

Gradually their initial fervor lessened and they rolled about on the bearskin in a tangle of legs and arms. Almost before they began, Thad's enforced countenance betrayed him and he exploded in a myriad of bright pieces.

"Oh . . . oh . . . aaaaah!" he cried out, abandoning the sweet pleasure of her welcoming nest for the first time.

Rebecca shuddered through her completion and they lay side by side on the black fur. "Marvelous. You are simply marvelous, Thad," she whispered.

"And so are you. I . . . I'd forgotten how much . . . I . . ."

"Don't be shy about it. How much you enjoyed it. That's only the beginning, my darling Thad. See? Already you are rising to the occasion."

Rebecca reached downward and grasped his smooth flesh. It stiffened at her touch and new fires kindled in his groin. Gently, she drew him to her, and they joined together once again.

Thad entered her in a rush, sending shivers along both their backs. He drew back slowly, paused until she begged for more, then plunged forward once again. Rebecca arched her back and came up to meet him. She shuddered with maddening sensations of paradise and locked her strong legs round his waist. Thad's pace increased and the world whirled away.

Sometime, it must have been before their fourth or fifth amorous engagement, they got up and went into the bedroom. Rebecca recalled groggily that she had never made love on a bearskin before. It had been, all considered, one of the most stimulating experiences of her life.

Chapter 15

"The snows are melting. You'll be going soon."

"Yes. I must. There's so much to be done, Thad."

Rebecca Caldwell and Thad Walsh lay naked in the big iron poster bed in the cabin. Jamie was outside, playing in the sparkling sunlight. He made snowballs and threw them, yelling and giggling with glee. His little sister lay asleep in the loft, taking her afternoon nap. Three days had passed since their first glorious night on the bearskin before the fire. On this sparkling afternoon, they had made love for the second time only moments before and now basked in the happy glow of their fading emotions.

"I don't want you to. You know that."

"Yes. I love being here like this with you beside me. The children. Caring for them. Making love with you."

"Morning, noon, and night, I might add," Thad inserted.

"I've not heard you object."

"We're not talking about me. It's you. You're insatiable. My wife was like that. I've been lucky, I suppose. White women are so reserved, so . . . put off by something that can be so darned much fun. Indian women are . . ."

139

"Lusty? Yes, of course. And not a bit ashamed of it, either. Come here, you wonderful man, and let me show you how lusty we can be."

Rebecca grabbed at him and Thad yelped in mock alarm. "Have mercy, woman. I'll not have strength to chop wood."

"Who needs wood? The snow *is* going away. Winter's a long way off. Come to me, before I devour you where you lay."

"I'd like that."

"You're too willing."

Eyes locked on his, Rebecca rose to her knees and straddled Thad's supine form. Slowly she lowered herself. Thad reached for her hips and she squirmed away.

"Hurry," Thad urged. "Jamie might come in."

"Let him. He already knows all about us. He told me he watched from the loft when we were on the bearskin. He thought it looked funny.

"Why, that little scudder. I'll warm his behind for that."

"No you won't. We'll just make certain he doesn't have a front row seat the next time."

With a determined push, Rebecca plunged Thad's manhood deep within her. She churned her hips and lay back against his upraised knees. Throwing back her head, she hummed tunelessly as bolts of pleasure crashed resoundingly through her fevered body. How good, how truly good Thad was as a lover. She marveled at his endurance. Prolong it, she cautioned. It would all end far too soon . . .

*   *   *

"There's two men comin'," Jamie announced from the doorway.

Rebecca stood at the stove, frying a skilletful of disjointed woodcock that Thad had shot that afternoon. She looked up from her work to where the man she had loved so unrestrainedly for the past five days sat in his rocker.

"Neighbors?"

"Not likely. Nearest whites are ten miles off. Could it be that friend of yours you told me about?"

"If it is . . ."

"You'll be leaving," Thad said sadly.

"Yes, Thad. Oh, I don't want to. But we do have to hurry now. Time has run out on that week the Nez Percé gave Lone Wolf and me." Anguish colored Rebecca's words. "There just can't be a war. It would destroy them all."

"I know. And my brother-in-law would be right there in the forefront fighting the whites."

"Jamie, go out and see what the men look like," Rebecca took the initiative. "Then come tell me."

"Sure, Becky," he chirped.

"I'll miss you," Thad began.

"No. Don't say our good-byes until we have to. It might not be Lone Wolf."

"It had better be. The only other whites out here alone like that are the outlaws you're after."

"Them I can take care of."

"I believe you. You have told me so much of your adventures since that son of a b . . . forgive me . . . before Jake Tulley and your uncles traded you off to the Sioux. I have no doubts about that. What I wonder is . . . ?"

141

"Yes," Rebecca asked breathlessly, part of her mind already excited beyond bounds by visions of the next delicious time they would lay together in the bed. "What is it?"

"I wonder if you are able to finish this thing alone? You or even the two of you. What I mean is . . . if you'll have me along, I want to help."

"But the children?"

"They can stay with neighbors. Or I can take them to my wife's family at Wallowa Valley."

"Oh . . . Thad. I . . ." Memories of other men who had loved her dearly and fought at her side, only to die or be horribly maimed, crowded her thoughts and emotions. "It's dangerous."

"And you are there."

"There's no guarantee we can win."

"But you fight on."

"You don't know how terrible it is to fight against Roger and see him slip away."

"If you seek him for an eternity, I want to be at your side."

"You could be killed."

"I'd die gladly in your arms."

"Oh, Thad! Thad, this is foolish. Like moonstruck children. Please, please listen to me."

"Only if you tell me you love me."

"I do . . . but this is about the danger we're going into. If we fail, if I don't find Lone Wolf and stop Roger from stealing the *Cho-pun-nish* horses, then there will be war."

"And I've already been told that some among the tribe want me dead and the children raised in a *Cho-pun-nish* village. So, what risk that I don't already take?"

"Poppa! Becky!" Jamie interrupted, breathlessly. "I

142

ran to the end of our clearing to look. It's a big, strong man, dressed like an Indian. He has yellow hair."

"Lone Wolf! He's come. Who's with him?"

"An old man," Jamie replied without interest. "He comes here once in a while."

"Old Salty?" Thad inquired, surprised.

"That's him," Jamie confirmed.

"Oh, let's go out and meet them," Rebecca enthused. "I can broil some salmon to make enough. They'll be tired and worried about me. Now we can celebrate."

"Only if you agree that I can come along. At least until we see how this will eventually go."

"Oooh! Yes," Rebecca gushed suddenly. "Yes, dearest Thad. Come along if you must. I . . . can't bear parting from you so soon."

". . . and so, I wandered around until Salty found me," Lone Wolf concluded as the four adults sat over coffee after a filling meal.

"What made you come this way?"

Lone Wolf flushed. "I can't say I was drawn to find you in these parts. I figured that the survivors of the gang would be wandering around in the area. So Salty and I decided to take up sniping on them. The noise of a gun battle should attract you if you're nearby, I figured. That way we could do two things at once."

"Hummm. I don't know if I should let that one go or not." Rebecca affected a mock pout.

"Here now," Lone Wolf made pained protest.

"Thad says you darn near froze in that blizzard," Salty put in to change the subject.

"I did. For the longest time I saw no sign of another

person or any secure shelter."

Over the next twenty minutes, Rebecca outlined what had occurred since she and Lone Wolf had been separated. She omitted the wonderful hours she and Thad had spent in bed. She figured that from her rosy glow, Lone Wolf would know well enough. When she concluded, Thad opened the door to more protest when he announced his intention.

"You can't do it. It's too dangerous. Who would look after your children if something happened?" Lone Wolf exploded. He covered all the objections Rebecca had come up with and more. Thad only smiled blandly and countered every one.

In the end, Lone Wolf and Salty agreed with the youthful pair and wished Thad well in joining their enterprise.

Within two days after leaving Jamie and Elizabeth at the nearest neighbor's homestead, Rebecca and the three men with her came across ample signs of the outlaws and their latest bag of stolen Palouse horses. Lone Wolf scouted ahead, while Rebecca and the others laid plans for an attack.

"We have to finish them all if possible," Rebecca declared.

Thad gave her an odd look. Hearing about her long trail of vengeance and bloodshed while lying supine and weak from spent passion might be one thing. Now, to hear her coldly plot the murder of some fifteen men chilled his blood.

"We'll turn their own tactics against them. We three will move in and kill any sentries they have out, then

Lone Wolf will make a direct attack. We'll follow him in from three sides and keep the pressure on the gang while he makes off with the horses. Then, a final clean sweep and we pull away."

"What if there's survivors?" Salty inquired.

"We question them about Roger, then finish them off."

Thad winced. "What if one of us is hurt?"

"The others will do everything to make sure the wounded one is safe. We won't even leave them a body to identify."

"An' iffin ol' Roger, Fancy Dan, Styles is with 'em?"

Rebecca grinned nastily at Salty. "I get him personally. There's a lot he has to pay for."

"You'll find out about that within two hours," Lone Wolf stated as he strode into the illumination of their campfire. "The gang and the horses they stole are bedded down about an hour's ride from here."

Chapter 16

Restless, Roger Styles slept lightly. Tossing and turning, he hovered at the edge of consciousness. In that hazy state, his mind received and interpreted sounds that went unremarked by others in the slumbering camp.

A click. Was it a hammer being cocked?

A picketed horse stamped the ground and shuffled in annoyance. Did someone approach stealthily by way of their saddle mounts?

The clash of what could only be the lever action of a Winchester rifle.

"Whatwasthat?" Roger came awake so abruptly that fragments of his dreamlike memories veiled clear thinking.

He swung his bare shanks over the side of the folding cot and bent to search for his boots. A moment later, his confused sense impressions gained validity as a shot blasted the night apart.

From the direction of the cook fire ring, a man began to scream. Hideous sounds came from his raw throat in testimony to the cruelty of the blaze into which he had fallen.

"Up! Everybody up!" Roger shouted needlessly.

"We're being attacked."

In a disjointed swirl, the outlaws came out of their blankets, grabbing for trousers and boots, encumbered by the weapons they picked up first. Yellow-orange flame stabbed the darkness again, and one of the rustlers cried out in agony, clutching his thigh.

"Get moving, get moving. They're over by the horses." A sort of prescience guided Roger's tactics. His sleeping impressions had been given form and substance. He scrambled from his tent with a cocked revolver in his right hand.

"They're all around us," Lew Gorce informed him.

"How many?"

"I don't know, Roger. Maybe a dozen, might be less. Only a couple of shots. In this dark you can bet that whoever fired them ain't where he was when he did."

"We have enough men to flush them out. Get them into some sort of order and go after the bastards out there."

Rebecca Caldwell approached the camp with the practiced stealth of a Sioux warrior. Despite this, the outlaws' horses soon sensed her presence and began to pull on their picket rope. One of them snorted and stomped the ground. At least their restiveness helped her keep on course through the starless night.

Clouds had returned with sunset and cloaked the forest land in stygian velvet. Rebecca progressed toward the rustlers' camp with one arm extended, fingers probing like a blind man. Her other hand held her Winchester saddle carbine. It would get good use this night, she promised herself. Unexpectedly, the trees

147

ended. Rebecca stood on the edge of a small glade, the tied horses forming darker lumps against the blackness. She counted to fifty, as her plan called for, to let the others get into position. Then she worked her Winchester action quietly as possible.

"Whatwasthat?" Muffled words, strung together so that they became indistinct, came to her from a tent close at hand.

A moment later, a pinpoint of light flared and blossomed into a tiny blaze as one of the guards struck a lucifer to ignite the morning cook fire. As the flame ate at the wood, his body distinguished itself in silhouette against the yellow-red tongues licking beyond him.

"Turn around," Rebecca hissed between clinched teeth as she sighted on his back. Badmen they might be, but she was loath to backshoot anyone.

Unable to hear her muffled urging, the man nevertheless turned outward to the blackness, blinking eyes rendered temporarily sightless by the fire. Rebecca squeezed the trigger.

The blast covered his soft grunt as a hot .44-40 slug punched into his belly. He bent double, then fell backward, sprawled in the fire. His hair and shirt caught fire instantly and he began to scream in agonized horror. Shouted questions rose from the sleeping forms of the outlaws. Above the tumult, Rebecca recognized Roger Styles's voice as he bellowed for everyone to repel the attack. Then another Winchester cracked from a quarter-way around the camp.

Thad Walsh, Rebecca thought fondly. Despite the fervor of the attack and the danger she faced, her loins still tingled with memory of his ample and expert loving. She saw his target go down, hands clasped to a spurting wound in one thigh. Hit the artery, she thought. Chances were, she knew, the wounded hard case would not live another five minutes. From the other two sides, Lone Wolf and Old Salty—both armed with Spencer repeaters—added bass booms to the fury of incoming fire.

A short, scrawny rustler flew off his feet and smashed against a tree.

"Gaa-gaaa-goddamn, I'm hit," he gurgled, drowning on blood that poured into his lungs from the ragged .52 caliber hole in his throat.

Another of Roger's gunhawks managed to get off a round in the direction from which Thad had fired before a sizzling Spencer round dumped him off his feet. Rebecca stepped back and to her right. She took her curved-bladed skinning knife from the scabbard at her waist and cut the picket rope. Then she loosed a round skyward from the Winchester directly in front of the muzzles of the wall-eyed horses.

Instantly, the outlaws' mounts bolted. Whinnying in fright, they thundered away into the utter darkness. Quickly, Rebecca ran to her left and stopped at a new vantage point. The Winchester came to her shoulder.

How had the bloody sods managed to get so close to them? Clive Reversford pondered his unspoken rhetorical question as he scrambled, half-clad, from his tent.

He shivered in the chill night and his hand trembled as he attempted to loosen his revolver in its holster. The awkward, unbalanced Webley fired a shorter cartridge than the .45 Colt, with considerably less range and accuracy. All the same, Clive would be damned before he let himself go down without some show of resistance. He fired blindly into the darkness. A pounding of hoofs close by and the wild neighing of the frightened animals jerked his attention in a new direction.

"Good Lord, they've cut loose our horses!" he shouted.

"They'll go after the ones we stole next," Roger yelled at him from the opposite side of camp.

"Too late for that," Clem Dye hollered from the edge of the clearing. "They've already run them off."

The screaming from the firepit stopped. Peering toward the milling saddle horses, Clive saw a figure, illuminated by the burning corpse. He threw a shot from his Webley, which missed.

Flame bloomed at the muzzle of the rifle in the dark figure's hands. A drop forge smashed into Clive's chest and sent him staggering backward. For a moment the fire cast light on the face of the person who had shot him.

"By gahd!" he exclaimed weakly. "It's a woman whose done for me." His vision dimmed even faster than the light.

Coughing blood, Clive Reversford let the Webley slip from numb fingers. He sat abruptly and clasped one hand over the wound in the left side of his chest.

"A bloody damned woman," he said again, wonderingly. Then Clive keeled over on his left side, legs and arms trembling with his death throes, and watched the lights go out forever.

"We made the withdrawal just in time," Lone Wolf observed as he trotted along with his companions behind the string of Palouse horses they drove back toward the Salmon River.

"Yes. Roger and the gang had nearly recovered from

our surprise. It burns me, though, to not have finished Roger as a bonus," Rebecca responded.

"White Goose is going to be happy about getting these ponies back," Thad Walsh remarked. "It may be enough to keep *Wahlitits* from having his way."

"We can't count on that," Rebecca commented glumly. "How far have we to go?"

"Another ten miles or so," Thad told her.

Great excitement filled the villages of the Tepahlewan Canyon when the spotted-rump horses appeared. Driven by two white men well known to the *Cho-pun-nish*, and the Sioux warrior woman *Šinaskawin*, along with her friend of the *Absaroka*, the eighty Palouse horses trotted smartly through the first clan encampment, heads high and eyes bright. Children shouted shrilly and ran alongside. At the longhouse of *Peopeo Kiskiak Hihi*, the council had gathered. They stood silent, unmoving, while young men and boys took over the horses and herded them to pasture.

"You have done well," the headman declared in ringing tones.

"Thank you," Thad said quietly.

"The men who took our horses . . . what has become of them?"

"Some are dead. Many fled in fear. They will not come raiding again," Rebecca promised. "A few escaped unharmed. Among them the man responsible, Roger Styles. We'll return now to Pendleton and free the remaining horses. If anyone gets in our way, they will have to accept the consequences."

A wry smile lit White Goose's face. "For one who speaks so strongly for peace, you talk war with great ferocity."

"My fight with the man called Styles is an old one,

White Goose. I'll not rest 'till I slay him."

"Or he ends your life, daughter."

"You have enough years to deserve to be called Grandfather, yet have any of your enemies killed you?"

"Oho! She speaks with the tongue of a headman. Come, refresh yourselves. There will be feasting tonight for the return of our ponies."

"We want to go after the rest, and to catch Roger Styles. But we cannot refuse such generous hospitality," Rebecca told the sixty-nine year old chief, her tone alive with flirtation.

"It was that goddamned bitch, I tell you," Roger Styles railed at Lew Gorce. "It had to be Rebecca Caldwell. Those stupid Indians would never have thought to attack like that. Or to withdraw the moment we began to recover and return effective fire."

"You're probably right," Gorce allowed. "They hit us hard, took back them Appaloosies, and got clean away."

"Worse, they killed Clive Reversford. He was starting to be quite likable. And I'm out a partner."

"What now? That bunch can't be ever'where at once. There's lots more Appaloosies out here for the takin'."

"I'm tempted to hit at Wallowa Valley on our way to Pendleton."

"Remember what Sheriff Holman told you, Roger. That could lead to trouble with the state."

"Yes, dammit. And that's the reason we won't. So, we ride like hell for home and hope we beat Rebecca Caldwell there."

"You think she'll go after the rest we have corralled?"

"That you can count on absolutely. Look at us. The

152

gang's broken, scattered. We have five men left, counting you, Lew. The rest run off or dead. She's going to know that. So she'll come after the Appaloosies."

"And we'll be waitin', right?"

"Exactly. Only we have to be clever, Lew. Much more so than we've been until now. At every encounter, she's gotten the upper hand. From here on, that stops. We're going to cook up a little trap for Rebecca Caldwell."

Chapter 17

Objects stood out in sharp relief. The air held that fragile luminosity typical of autumn after the departure of Indian summer. Most of the leaves had been stripped from the alders by the untimely blizzard. Those that remained had changed from bright yellows and orange to dismal brown. The forest seemed hushed, as though holding its breath, and the riders halted at a fork in the trail.

"We'll divide here," Rebecca Caldwell instructed her companions. "You and Salty go north and west; we'll bear to the south. Warn everyone you can. And hurry."

"I reckon we've got less time than we need," Salty remarked.

"Dang that young hothead. You'd think what we'd done would be appreciated."

"It was," Lone Wolf declared. "White Goose has come to the same conclusion we did. *Wahlitits* is using the horse stealing as an excuse. He wants war with the whites no matter what the circumstances."

There had been feasting aplenty in the Tepahlewan Canyon villages. For a second time, horses stolen by the whites had been returned. This time, those responsible

154

had been killed or run off. The singers made up songs about the bravery of the Sioux girl, *Šinaskawin*, and her courageous friends. The festive mood had been dampened, though, when *Wahlitits* and a dozen of his followers arrived.

It didn't matter, *Wahlitits* declared, that the rustling had stopped. Revenge had to be exacted. He called for all true *Cho-pun-nish* warriors to join him in raids on the whites. The week of truce had ended. Now they would make the white men feel the sharpness of their arrows. Ten youthful malcontents joined him. Preparations began for the warpath.

While the twenty-three braves painted for battle, Rebecca and the three men with her held a hurried conference with White Goose. The old headman agreed that some warning had to be given. So far everything had gone as Rebecca had promised. There had to be time for it to work. He offered to send messengers to the other bands and alert the chiefs of the impending raids. They could hold most of their people in check. It would be up to Rebecca, Lone Wolf, Thad, and Salty to spread word to the whites. Saddened by this turn and impatient to pursue Roger to Pendleton, the four rode out before daybreak.

"We'll travel in a zigzag pattern, working closer to Pendleton all the while," Rebecca added. "When Thad and I get to Wallowa Valley, we can hopefully prevail on Chief Joseph to hold *Wahlitits* and his followers there. At least long enough to insure there is no killing of whites."

"We can't reach everyone," Thad reminded her. "There are some people in these mountains who don't want to be found. If *Wahlitits* comes on them, they'll get no mercy."

"We'll do our best," Rebecca answered sternly.

The tip of his pen knife rattled impatiently in the brass keyhole of the lock on the rolltop desk. Jason Brill sweated heavily as he struggled to spring the bolt and allow him access to the secrets in the pigeonholes under the curved cover. He had already appropriated Roger' account in his bank and had a look in the tin lockbox in the vault. The results had been disappointing. There had to be more and better, the greedy little banker swore.

To forward his quest, he had bided time. Word had gone around town that Roger and his men had been killed by Indians. One survivor of the attack had spent a night in Pendleton, drank a lot, and talked freely, before he hurried on toward the south and safety in Portland. After three more days, the banker used the cover of night to enter the office and begin his search.

Brill was doomed to disappointment, though. A hidden safe, of which he was entirely unaware, and not the vulnerable desk, contained Roger's secrets. Brill's jowls quivered as he exerted renewed effort.

There! He almost had it.

A loud bang announced the opening of the front door. Jason Brill quivered in terror and turned his frightened deep-set eyes toward the entrance.

Roger Styles stood there, full of life, fists on his hips, legs wide apart. A scornful sneer twisted his full sensuous lips downward. Contempt illuminated his smokey gray eyes from far within. Without a word, he stalked across the smooth plank floor.

Jason Brill licked his thin, disapproving lips and tugged nervously at the lobe of one small, cup-handle ear. His receding chin quavered as he worked to form words.

"Ah . . . well, Roger! It's good to see you. I . . . we, ah, heard that you had been murdered by the savages. I, ah, naturally wanted to be of what aid I could in organizing your affairs. In the event there were heirs, naturally."

Acid coated every syllable of Roger's reply. "Jason, my friend and partner. If I didn't know you so well, I could swear that when I came in, you were trying to force the lock on my desk."

"Uh . . . no! Why would I do a thing like that?" Brill's protest of innocence came too fast.

"Why indeed? Since, as you can see, I am quite alive and well. You, ah, wouldn't happen to have sequestered my bank account, would you? All in the name of preserving it for my heirs, of course."

"Roger . . . I . . . I can explain . . ."

Roger's sarcasm cut like a razor. "Oh, I'm sure you can. Jason, if I didn't need you, need the services of your bank to carry off my horse-selling plan, I'd blow your slimy little brain out the back of your head right where you stand. Bankers!" He spat the word like a gobbet of offal. "Along with lawyers and doctors, bankers are the biggest charlatans and the foulest crooks on the face of the earth. From here on, you do exactly and only what I say. Do I make myself clear on that?"

Brill nodded feebly. "Er . . . ah . . . how is it that you didn't show up here sooner? What happened?"

"Oh, the boys who stayed with me are around, right enough. We've been watching the corrals from hidden places outside of town.

"But why?"

"We've set a little trap for Rebecca Caldwell. There's three things Rebecca loves to the point of distraction:

157

children, Indians of any sort, and sex. Since we haven't a nice young man to dangle in front of her, and there aren't any children who need rescuing, we have to be satisfied with her attraction to Indians. We're baiting our trap with all those horses out there. She'll come, because retrieving those Appaloosies will make her Indian friends happy. Then . . . then we have her right where I want her. Now, get out of here, you lard-bellied little weasel."

Brill worked his mouth, but said nothing. Scuttling sideways, he skirted Roger and made for the door.

"And . . . ah . . . Jason, by tomorrow morning I want all my money and papers back where they belong."

Seven settlers had been warned by the time Rebecca and Thad made camp for the night. Hot, tired, and dusty, Rebecca suggested a bath in the chill stream that meandered through the meadow where they rested. Thad eagerly agreed.

Their ablutions washed away grime and fatigue. Before long their ardor began to rise. Unfortunately, icy water proved no inducement to erotic ambitions. Eager to find again the rapture of their commingling, Rebecca started for the bank.

Once there, she wrapped them both in a large, absorbent blanket. Rebecca thrilled to the silken touch of his skin against hers. Thad bent his head and kissed her fervently. His hardness pressed against her taut abdomen and she hurried to grasp it in strong, knowing fingers.

Rebecca sighed with contentment as she began to stroke Thad's ample maleness. Their kiss ended and Thad began to nuzzle his lips in the hollow of her throat. One of

158

his strong, calloused hands cupped her right breast and a sure thumb began to knead the nipple into surging erectness.

"Aaah," Rebecca breathed out. "How I've ached for you, my darling Thad. I thought I would go mad with need."

"I've been in agony wanting you," Thad admitted.

Over his shoulder, Rebecca spotted a large, stout limb of a birch that hung down like a smoothly polished wooden saddle, its upper surface about hip-high to Thad. She pointed to it and turned Thad's head.

"There. Over on that branch. I want to pad it with the blanket and sit on it. Then you can make wild, fierce love to me."

Intrigued by this unorthodox position, Thad joined in gladly. Rebecca seated herself and leaned back, braced by her arms. She spread her legs widely, inviting Thad's inspection of her treasures. Excited as a young boy, Thad stepped in closer.

Shivers of ecstasy rippled over Rebecca's skin as they came together in glorious fury. Her heart pounded and infinite explosions of pure pleasure consumed her brain.

Rebecca wrapped her long, shapely legs around his waist and clung to him with all her might.

On raged their amorous combat, the contestants lost to an oblivion of rapture. Steadying their pace, they abandoned their enjoyment. At last, consumed in their self-kindled conflagration, they burst together into blazing, multicolored pinwheels of untrammeled delight.

"Oh-oh, how wonderful, Thad," Rebecca panted when reason returned. "Let's don't even bother to dress. I

159

want to eat and get back to the essentials. I don't want to end this night ever. Oh, my love, how greatly you thrill me. And there will be more . . . and more . . . and more . . . until the sun rises tomorrow."

"Let tomorrow never come," Thad murmured as he bent forward to nibble at her silken skin.

"Again? Now? Oh, yes, Thad. Yes!"

Chapter 18

Rebecca and Thad came upon the stockade unexpectedly, around noon the next day. Above the pointed pole ramparts of the small outpost, the bright colors of the American flag rippled in a steady breeze. The cadenced voice of a drill instructor could be heard chanting from inside. The pair halted and studied the situation.

"That wasn't here a year ago," Thad remarked. A frown creased his high, clear brow. "General Howard is moving his troops closer to Wallowa Valley all the time. No wonder men like *Wahlitits* shout for war."

"We have to go let them know," Rebecca stated the obvious.

"But I don't have to like it . . . or them," Thad grumbled in acknowledgement.

Smiling at this revelation of his loyalties, Rebecca reached over and patted his hand. "Think how much faster the message will get to settlers with the soldiers doing the riding. That lets us go directly to Pendleton without need to warn any except those directly in our path."

"You think of everything," Thad admitted.

"Flattery will get you nowhere. Let's ride in. Maybe

161

they'll even buy us dinner."

Officers and enlisted men ate together on so small a post. A line had already formed at the mess hall when Rebecca and Thad halted their horses at the tie-rail in front of the headquarters building. Commanded by a first lieutenant, Primus Clark, the garrison consisted of thirty privates, six noncoms, and two officers. The troop sergeant, Colin O'Donnel, escorted Rebecca into Lieutenant Clark's office.

"What is it we can do for you, Miss?" Primus Clark inquired. He eyed Rebecca's elkhide dress coldly.

"Some of the Nez Percé are up in arms over a series of murders committed by white men and the theft of many of their horses," Rebecca began. "The young men, urged on by a warrior named *Wahlitits*, are seeking to avenge the killings of some boys and men and the thefts by attacking white settlers. The people of the area must be warned and brought to some place of protection."

"You're not a Nez Percé," Lieutenant Clark began in a tone cloaked in suspicion. "I would judge, though, that your sympathies lie with the savages."

Rebecca gave him a flat-toned recital of facts too often explained. "The dress is Sioux. Oglala to be exact. I was a captive for five years and came to find this type of clothing preferable to more restrictive and uncomfortable white women's dress. I wouldn't be here if I didn't have the interests of the white settlers at heart."

"All the same, why did you take this all on yourself?"

"Because I happened to be present in the Tepahlewan band when *Wahlitits* raised the pipe for war. There are three others who were there also. Thad Walsh, who is outside; Brett Baylor, a friend of mine; and a resident of Pendleton, Clement Salters."

"Old Salty?" Lieutenant Clark inquired.

"The same."

"Well now, this seems more probable now that you mention him. Did you bring along any proof that an uprising is imminent?"

"No. Besides, it's not an uprising, Lieutenant. *Wahlitits* and twenty-two young men, some mere boys of sixteen or so, are going to attack isolated homesteads and kill whites. All of the headmen spoke for peace."

"We know *Wahlitits* quite well," Clark informed her. He stroked his full, blond mustache and continued to eye Rebecca with doubt. "He's a renegade and a trouble-maker. I'll get a message off to General Howard, of course. Then I shall take my troops into the field, round up *Wahlitits* and his followers, and take them to Department Headquarters. There the murdering scum will be hanged."

"That's preposterous!" Rebecca flared. "If you send men to warn the settlers, there won't be any 'murdering' going on by *Wahlitits* or anyone else."

"I can't spare any men for that. I'll need every one to apprehend these hostiles and get them to Fort Vancouver to be executed."

Anger boiled now, close to the surface. "Do you have a hearing problem, Lieutenant Clark, or is it low intelligence? It's an elemental thing. Watch my lips if you have to. If the settlers are temporarily removed, there will be no killings and no cause for executions."

"These Nez Percé are *hostiles*, Miss Caldwell, vermin. And like vermin, they should be exterminated to the last man, woman, and child."

"Oh, you're a fine one to be put in charge of an outpost in the middle of Indian country. I suppose you heartily subscribe to the sick philosophy of that blood-thirsty bastard, William Sherman."

"That '. . . The more we can kill this year, the less will have to be killed in the next war?' Yes. I most assuredly do. General Sherman was right. So was Custer. 'Nits make lice.' I would start with killing the children. That way we soon would not be bothered with these useless lumps of subhumanity."

"By God, you make me sick! You claim to be an officer of the United States Army, yet you think and act more like Attila the Hun. If you aren't going to warn the settlers, Thad and I will do what we can."

"No you won't," Lieutenant Clark told her in a hard, cold voice. "You are not to be spreading wild alarms of unsubstantiated dangers. In order to prevent it, I'm prepared to lock you in the guard house. That way, tranquility can be maintained among the settlers."

Astounded, Rebecca could only gasp. It took a moment for her to regain her composure enough to speak. "You *want* them to be massacred. Is that it, Lieutenant? You want enough settlers butchered to justify the extermination of not only a few reckless youths but the entire Nez Percé nation."

A cold, supercilious smile spread on Lieutanant Clark's face. "I couldn't have expressed it any better myself. Yes, Miss Caldwell. It is high time these unruly, disobedient savages learn their lesson. For more than ten years, they have refused to go on the reservation . . . so they must die. I'll not have such a prime opportunity taken from my grasp by an unfortunate warning that could prevent the situation from going critical. After all, if the Nez Percé won't abide by their own treaty, what can they expect?"

Could he really mean what he was saying? Surely Clark's attitude didn't reflect that of his superiors? Speechless, Rebecca seriously considered grabbing into her beaded squaw bag for the .38 Baby Russian and finishing this evil man before he could effect his horrible plot. In her moment of hesitation, Lieutenant Clark turned slightly and raised his voice.

"Sergeant O'Donnel."

The troop sergeant entered with a crash of boots on raw boards and snapped out a sharp salute. "Yes, sir! What is it you wish, sir?"

"Escort this young woman, and the gentleman in the outside office, to the provost. They are to be confined under protective custody until the troops return."

"If I may ask, sir, return from where?"

Clark produced a boyish grin. "We're going out to kill a few heathen redskins, Sergeant."

"Sure an' the boys'll be lovin' that, sir."

"I'll cut the orders at once. See to the protection of these nice folks, will you?"

"Yes, sir."

Thad Walsh made the mistake of resisting.

"Where is he taking us?" he inquired when he and Rebecca reached the parade ground.

"The good lieutenant wants to start a nice little Indian war. We're to be locked in the guard house so he can have his way."

"He will like hell," Thad blurted.

Thad reached out for Sergeant O'Donnel's shoulder and yanked the burly Irishman around. He got a hard left fist in the side of his head for his effort. Staggering, Thad

165

got his guard up in time to slip off the next pair of blows. Then he tagged O'Donnel with a short, hard right under the heart.

The punch stunned O'Donnel for a moment. Thad moved in and cracked knuckles off the thick neck of the troop sergeant. O'Donnel backpedaled, arms windmilling. Then his face suffused with dark crimson rage. A fine madness, as his countrymen would call it, overcame him and he plowed back into the fight.

Chin tucked in, shoulders high and rolling, O'Donnel snorted like a rutting bull and shuffled in close, absorbing all Thad had to give. Then he began to piston his arms, right-left, right-left, punishing Thad's rib cage. Out of breath, Thad tried to dance back. O'Donnel followed.

A sharp right cross twisted Thad's head to the side. O'Donnel's savage left hook lifted the slighter man off his feet. Thad struck the hard-packed parade ground with a grunt. He shook his head with an effort, trying to clear it. O'Donnel stepped in close and kicked Thad in the head.

"Thompson, Doolin!" O'Donnel panted out to a pair of privates standing in the shade of the sutler's porch. "Front and center."

The troopers trotted over and formed up in front of the burly NCO. "Now, lads. It seems this gentl'man fell and had hisself an accident. I wants yez to carry him to the guard house. I'll see to escortin' the young lady."

Gloom tugged at Rebecca's spirit. She and Thad, still unconscious, had been locked in a single, large, crudely constructed cell behind the bunkroom and office of the provost. A trumpeter had sounded assembly and the

166

troops formed up on the parade ground. Half an hour later, some mounted, the remainder on foot, they departed to seek out the Nez Percé. That left a young second lieutenant, Edward Andrews, in charge of a dozen men. Thad groaned and Rebecca abandoned her dolorous vigil at the small, barred window.

"Wha-what did he hit me with?" Thad croaked, dry-throated.

"The good sergeant kicked you in the head. If it would have done any good, I'd have shot him down like a dog."

"You had a gun with you?"

"Still do." Rebecca smiled conspiratorially and patted her beaded squaw purse that hung from the slim belt around her waist. "Even our bloodthirsty Sergeant O'Donnel balked at searching a woman. What we have to do now is figure a way to get out of here."

"I place our chances somewhere between slim and none," Thad replied. His color had returned and he made a weak attempt to sit up.

"Lay back there. Nothing's to be gained by forcing yourself right now. Some of these young soldiers don't look too experienced. If we could entice one of them in here . . ." Rebecca began planning aloud.

An hour went by with one idea after another being expounded and rejected. Rebecca began to suspect they would never hit on the right scheme. Their rumbling stomachs reminded them that the Army had never provided the meal they expected. Outside, the diminished routine of the outpost went on, seemingly oblivious of the prisoners.

"What do you think will happen to us when Lieutenant Clark returns?" Thad speculated aloud.

"He'll probably arrange for some sort of fatal accident.

167

That doesn't mean we have to cooperate with him," Rebecca added to lighten the grim prediction.

"I'd rather not wait around that long. I suppose we're stuck with your original idea to lure a guard close enough to get the keys and break out that way. Right now, I'd settle for anything."

With a rattle and creak, the big door between the bunkroom and the cellblock swung open. Lt. Edward Andrews stood in the frame. Behind him a private held a large, heavily laden tray.

Dressed in a new, tight-fitting uniform, Ed Andrews had a boyish appearance, enhanced by his smooth, beardless face, unruly, close-cropped sandy hair, and a scatter of freckles under his wide, innocent blue eyes. Of medium stature, he held himself well, though his expression was one of unease. He gestured with a thumb hooked over his shoulder.

"It just occurred to me that you two probably haven't eaten since early morning. I brought you something from the mess hall."

"That's the first nice thing we've heard around here, Lieutenant," Rebecca told him candidly.

"I'm . . . sorry for that." Andrews stopped abruptly, then turned to the soldier behind him. "Take that in, Whipple, and then you are dismissed."

"Yes, sir."

After the soldier left, Andrews stepped closer to the bars. "If I had my way, I'd turn you both loose right now and wish you God's speed on your mission to warn the settlers."

"Why, Lieutenant, I am utterly overwhelmed," Rebecca goaded him, her blue marble eyes level on his. "I thought every soldier out here couldn't wait to wet his sabre with Nez Percé blood."

"Please, the name's Ed and I'm serious. I don't agree with anything Primus Clark is doing. But"—Andrews made a helpless gesture—"I'm only a fresh new second lieutenant, right out from the Point. My opinions don't count. Even so, were there a way, I'd see you free in a minute."

"Give us time to eat and we might work something out for you," Thad remarked.

"What's he mean?"

Rebecca smiled sweetly. "There might be a way to let us out, warn the settlers, and save your career in the process."

"I'm all for it. Yet, I don't understand how . . ."

Perversely inscrutable, Rebecca gave him a flicker of upturned lips and nodded toward the food. "I'm famished. After we eat, I'll explain it all."

Andrews waited, albeit impatiently. He talked of inconsequential things, of his impressions of the country and the Nez Percé. Their horses, he concluded, were the most beautiful he had ever seen. He allowed as how he had sent another dispatch rider to Fort Vancouver with a report of what had happened and urged General Howard to order Lieutenant Clark back to the outpost.

"It's not done properly through the chain of command. I couldn't, because there isn't time. But then, when the commander is in the field, I am in charge here, so *technically* it can be said to be correct. Now what did you have in mind to do?"

"Simple," Rebecca told him. "I have a small Smith and Wesson revolver here. We'd originally planned to call in someone from the guard room and force him to let us out. Now all we have to do is change places with you and go our way. You can claim that it was done at gunpoint. Since Sergeant O'Donnel didn't search me, it's actually his fault, isn't it? They can hardly blame you for his error."

Andrews grinned hugely. "I've wanted to get something on that smart-mouth since I got here. I know he's responsible for a number of equipment losses. He is brutal and intransigent with the men. I've heard rumors, though no one is willing to come forward, that he has murdered several Indian women over the time the unit has been stationed here. He also wastes no opportunity to put me down in front of the troops. With this, I might get him some stockade time at Department Headquarters, or even Leavenworth. All right, when do we do it?"

"After dark would be best. Fewer people to see what happens. Only . . . the situation is too desperate for that."

"What about right now?" Andrews suggested.

"We'll do it that way," Rebecca agreed.

"Corporal of the guard, Post Number Two! Riders coming in."

"That's the gate guard. I wonder who it is?" Lieutenant Andrews speculated aloud.

"Whoever, it might provide the distraction we need to get away."

"You can always go out through the stable area and the pasture gate."

"Good. Let's get going then. Unlock the door and let's put you in here. Thad, you fix something to bind and gag the lieu . . . er, Ed. Then you're covered, I think."

Without further remarks, Ed Andrews took the ring of keys he held, unlocked the cell, and swung open the door. After Rebecca came out, he stepped inside. Thad quickly

170

ound his hands and feet and put a wadded-up piece of mattress ticking in Lieutenant Andrews's mouth. Then he stepped into the area between the dividing wall and the bars. Rebecca closed and locked the door.

"Good luck, Ed," she said in a kindly tone.

Rebecca and Thad retrieved their weapons and gear from the guard room. After a careful examination of the activity outside, they stepped from the office. Every man on the post had his attention fixed on the frightened-looking settlers who crowded at the gate. The fugitives turned sharply to the right and ran along the side of the building, screened by the one next to it. All they had left to do was cross the compound behind the officers' quarters, enter the stables, and get away on their horses.

A small task. Though a dangerous one.

Chapter 19

"They're out there rootin' in the ground like hog
after acorns," the civilian contract scout informed L
Primus Clark.

"Humm. Good. Gathering their obnoxious cama
bulbs, no doubt," the officer surmised. "How many c
them?"

"I make it out as twenty-five."

"Oh? I would expect more."

"This must be a small village. We're still a ways fro
Wallowa Valley, Lieutenant."

Clark made his decision swiftly, his voice somewha
petulant. "It's too good an opportunity to pass up
Sergeant O'Donnel."

"Sir!"

"Prepare the men to move out. We're going down t
do battle with some hostiles."

"Yes, sir. Off yer asses, me buckoes. Troops mount up
infantry form a line as skirmishers. We'll move out at
fast trot, mind, so be on yer toes, lads."

At a brisk pace, the soldiers, mostly on foot, ascende
the long, gradual reverse slope to a ridge overlooking th
valley. Below them, the Nez Percé women toiled a

172

gathering bulbs. After only a momentary hesitation, the troops surged down the opposite side, a rippling flow, like a blue tidal wave. Fixed bayonets winked evilly in the sun. In the lead, at the center, Lieutenant Clark waved his sabre in the air and let out a fearsome yell. All along the line, men took up the battle cry.

"Jesus God," Corp. Ian McDougal muttered to himself. "Did that crazy lieutanant bring us way out here to butcher women and children? That's not to my likin'. Or is it a feint to draw out their warriors? It's sure that's what I'm hopin' it's all about."

McDougal's hopes soon bore fruit. Though not exactly as he had envisioned it.

The sound of pounding hoofs alerted the Nez Percé women. Shouting the alarm, they abandoned their woven baskets and began to run. Lieutenant Clark reached the women first. He raised his sabre high to slash downward in what he anticipated would be a decapitating blow. An instant later, he howled with anguish and dropped his sword.

A hot slug smashed into the basket guard of Clark's sabre. Shards of lead and silver continued on, severely mangling the blood-lusting officer's right hand. He heard the crack of a rifle nearly on top of the beginning of enormous pain. Instantly he dropped his sabre. A moment later, Nez Percé warriors, mounted on galloping, handsome spotted-rump ponies appeared from all directions and rode swiftly inward, tightening a deadly ring around the soldiers.

Fully one hundred and twenty strong, they outnumbered the soldiers by four to one. Terror-edged surprise clouded Primus Clark's mind. Where had they come from? His scout had seen no sign of warriors. If he didn't

173

do something quickly, he and his men would be cornered and helpless, vastly outnumbered.

"Fire at will, men. Open fire!"

Springfield rifles spread a greasy smear of gray-white powder smoke over the scene of action. Hot lead streaked toward the attacking braves. From his vantage point, Lieutenant Clark saw a fat, mound-bellied warrior snap backward and do a flip over his mount's rump. Another Nez Percé cried out and fell away from the side of his pony. By then the war party had closed their circle and reduced its diameter by half.

"Dismount," Clark commanded. "The horses are of no use to us now."

An arrow thudded into the chest of his mount and it crashed to its knees, pitching the frantic young officer into the dusty grass. A soldier to his left cried out in agony and blood sprayed through the air. Primus Clark rolled over and surged to his feet.

When he came upright he found himself and his men tightly ringed by fierce-visaged warriors. For a long moment, neither side fired a shot. Clark stared, gape-mouthed, licking dry lips. A disturbance from behind set him spinning on one heel.

A tall, handsome Nez Percé, his chest covered by a bead-and-bone breastplate, shouldered his magnificent Palouse horse through the three-deep ring of warriors. He held a feathered war lance in one hand, a decorated shield in the other. Worked into his hair were the symbols of his office. He spoke in rich, well-modulated tones.

"You are seriously outnumbered, Lieutenant. Surely you don't wish to spend your lives foolishly?"

"You . . . you're Chief Joseph."

"That's what you whites call me, yes."

174

"How did . . . what made you? . . ."

"When we received word of soldiers on the move, I decided to set a little trap. My 'women,' as you have no doubt guessed by now, were actually young warriors in disguise. We wanted to see what your intentions were. Now, it seems, we have found out."

"I . . . it was all . . ."

"A mistake? I hardly think so. Don't concern yourself greatly, though. If you will all throw down your arms, we can end this peacefully. *We* do not make war on women, and we don't think highly of those who do. Regardless of this, we shall not kill you outright, nor save you for torture."

"What do you propose to do?" Clark's voice quavered slightly as he made a mental note of the number and armament of the Indians.

"Simply to march you to the soldier village of Fort Vancouver. There we will turn you over to the soldier chief, Howard. I think he will find this all most amusing."

"I don't think the general will see anything to laugh about."

"Hummm. You may be right. I understand he does not believe in making war on women and children either."

Clark winced at the reference. "We're hardly in a position to fight you. Yet, it's against regulations for us to surrender our arms voluntarily, or to provide same to any Indians."

"Oh, we'd give them back to you once we reached Fort Vancouver. All we wish to do is show our good faith to General Howard. To do that, we will escort you unarmed soldiers to the fort in order to protect you from *Wahlitits* and his renegades."

Unbounded humiliation sent deep color to Lt. Primus Clark's face. He could not meet the unflinching gaze of the powerful chief who confronted him. Slowly his eyelids closed and he shook his head sadly.

With the lethargy of a dream, Primus Clark reached across with his left hand and unfastened the buckle of his pistol belt.

Rebecca Caldwell reined in abruptly and Thad Walsh jolted to a halt beside her. With her left arm, Rebecca pointed in the direction they were headed.

"That's Old Salty coming, isn't it?"

Thad studied the jouncing figure who appeared from around a bend on a trotting mule. "It sure is. What's he doing headed our way?"

"We'll find out soon enough." Rebecca raised in her stirrups and hailed the old man. Then she set off at a canter.

"Jest the folks I was lookin' fer," Salty declared as the three joined up on the trail.

"Why's that?" Rebecca inquired.

"Yer friend, Lone Wolf, is headin' straight fer Pendleton. Wants to scout the area a bit. We done finished all the places I knew of. Folks is movin' to that new outpost the Army built. I figgered to hunt you up and we'd go on in. Time's a wastin'. That *Wahlitits* is supposed to be around here some place. So it's best if we get those horses outta Styles's corrals an' on their way home."

"If we managed to run the Palouses into *Wahlitits* and his war party, they'd be rather busy catching them up," Rebecca suggested mischievously.

176

Old Salty's eyes twinkled. "That shines!"

The trio rode on westward, toward Pendleton. Shortly after noon, Rebecca halted them again. From far in the distance, toward Wallowa Valley, they heard the faint thumps of gunfire. Rebecca pondered this a moment and scowled.

"That must be Lieutenant Clark and his soldiers," she suggested.

"Oh, word o' that got around, too. Seems as how *Hinmatooyahletkeht* fixed 'em up a little surprise. Don't imagine the good lieutenant will be in much of a mood for Injun fightin' for a spell after this."

"What's Chief Joseph have planned?"

"Not certain, but the way I heard it, it'll plumb embarrass the britches off that war-happy so'jer boy."

"Let's keep going. We've a lot of ground to cover." Rebecca suppressed her smile and gigged her horse into motion.

By late afternoon, only a scant five miles lay between the three riders and Pendleton. They had seen no sign of soldiers of *Wahlitits*'s war party.

So unexpected when it came, the shot startled them all. Thad's hat flew past Rebecca's face and she ducked at the crack of the bullet.

"Ambush!" she shouted and jumped her mount into a gallop. As more rifles opened on them, she veered to the right and streaked toward a large jumble of house-sized boulders some fifty yards from the road and a good hundred from their ambushers.

"In there," she cried, pointing forward. Thad and Salty quickly followed.

More rounds snapped past as they neared the shelter of the rocks. One slug smashed off a granite chunk and sprayed Thad's face with sharp-edged chips. Then Rebecca swung out of the saddle and ducked into the protection of their stone fortress. Thad and Old Salty came right behind her.

A thin-lipped, bloodless smile divided Red Ashton's face. Today he'd been put in charge of the ambush laid in the event Rebecca Caldwell and her friends came toward Pendleton along this road. A number of the stragglers had shown up in town and agreed to continue working for Styles. Roger had given them to Red and sent him out to secure the trail from the east. All together, he had eleven men. Enough, he figured. He sat upright and spat a toothpick from the corner of his mouth as three riders came into view over a slight rise.

One of them was sure female, all right. He could see the lovely swell of her tits even from that range. And her hair in braids. It fit the description Roger had given him. It didn't matter who the others might be. They'd all be dead in a matter of minutes. He raised his Winchester to his shoulder and gently squeezed the trigger.

Damn! The shot went wild. Just knocked the hat off the feller next to her. "Open up, boys. They're headin' for those rocks."

Three more rifles boomed. Red watched as the slugs went wide of their marks and cursed hotly. He slid down from his vantage point and started along the line of kneeling ambushers.

"We're gonna have to go after them. When I give the word, we'll charge."

* * *

It could be no one but Roger's men, Rebecca considered as she worked her way between boulders until she had a good view and an unobstructed field of fire. Right in time, too, she thought as men began to appear across the open field from them. In a ragged line, muzzles spouting flame and smoke, the outlaws rushed toward the disorganized heap of rocks. Rebecca eased her saddle carbine into position and took careful aim.

She winced slightly when the Winchester went off and its butt plate jolted into her shoulder. Out on the grassy stretch dirt kicked up between the legs of one hard case. He leaped to one side and nearly turned, only to be knocked to his knees by a round from Old Salty's Spencer. Good, Rebecca thought. Then she concentrated on another target.

Sy Burton. Rebecca put the name to the ugly face she saw in the sights. She drew a breath, let half out, then started her trigger squeeze.

Her bullet sped true. Sy Burton came to a sudden stop. His jaw hung slackly open and he weaved like a drunken man. Slowly he released his grip on an old Yellow Boy Winchester. It clattered to the ground. Sy gulped convulsively, groaned, and fell over. Dust rose as he kicked out his final death throes.

Only twenty yards between the defenders and Roger's gang. Rebecca had to do something fast and unexpected. She threw a quick shot at the short, redheaded man close to where she stood and saw a puff of cloth and blood spray from his left shoulder.

"Pull back!" Rad Ashton ordered. "Pull back."

While the others withdrew, Clem Dye and four of the

returned hard cases eased their way through the thick brush to one side of the defenders. When they reached the rocky hillside, Clem called them close. With a stout twig, he quickly sketched the defensive position.

"That gal an' her friends are hole' up like this. They got a good field of fire coverin' that meadow the boys has got to cross. An' they got plenty of cover because of the boulders. Thing is, they can't see to the sides much. What we're gonna do is crawl up through these rocks until we're above where they're settled in. Then," he concluded with a wicked grin, "we just pick ourselves some targets and start shootin'."

The climb upward proved to be a bit more than Clem had anticipated. Loose rocks threatened to come away and rattle down the slope, betraying their presence to the three defenders. A couple of the boys began to puff and gasp for air, unused to such hard physical activity afoot. Clem had to frequently look back, keeping check on them.

"Quiet," he cautioned over and over in a harsh whisper.

During one such admonishment, pain lanced up his leg as he made a misstep and twisted his ankle. He cursed foully under his breath and bit at his lip. Another fifty feet, he figured it, and they'd be ready to move across the slope. Gunfire crackled from below as Red and the rest set up harassing fire that whined and moaned off rounded hunks of rock. Progress slowed to a crawl.

"All right. That way . . . and spread out. Don't want our own boys pot-shottin' us," Clem directed.

For five tedious minutes both sides below traded shots. While they did, Clem and his men drew nearer to the designated spot. Bellies to the ground, they crawled over large mounds of stone until they could lift their heads and peer downward.

"There . . ." Clem breathed out quietly. "There they are." A note of triumph sounded even in the whisper.

Three backs presented easy targets as Clem motioned for everyone to take aim. Gently, he eased forward, settling his elbow in a pocket formed by smaller rocks.

The loud clatter came during a lull in firing. Thad jerked around quickly to stare upward at a dislodged rock that bounded down toward them. Beyond it he saw with chilling accuracy the faces of five men and the deadly muzzles of their weapons.

"Look out!" he shouted. "They're behind us."

Even as Rebecca and Old Salty sprang into motion, Thad brought his Winchester up and squeezed off in one smooth action. The slug sped uphill ahead of a puff of smoke. Along the ridge above, he watched in helplessness as flame spurted from five long guns.

One of them would never fire again, Thad thought with satisfaction. His hurried though accurate bullet smacked into Clem Dye's face, squarely between the eyes. Blood flew from Clem's ears and his head jerked backward. His rifle scraped noisily as it slid down the hill. Thad observed the effect of his bullet only a fraction of a second before he heard a meaty slap and soft groan from close by.

He turned to see Old Salty settle against the boulder in front of him like a deflating balloon. A crimson trickle began to seep from the round hole in the old man's back.

"Damn you! Damn you all," Thad screamed at the men above.

* * *

Quickly Rebecca responded to Thad's first warning shout. She wheeled and opened up with her Winchester. Even as an outlaw bullet punched into Old Salty's back, she rapidly cycled the lever action of her saddle carbine, sending one .44-40 slug after another screaming through the rocks. Thad soon joined in. Their combined fire quickly drove the surviving hard cases back from the ridge. They scrambled across the boulders and raced for the safety of their fellows beyond the meadow.

"They're on the run," Thad called gleefully. "I wish I'd got another one."

"I recognize the one you hit," Rebecca told him. "He was one of the leaders. We'd better check on Salty."

Rebecca knelt at the old man's side. His breathing was ragged. Tinges of gray-green showed in his pallid cheeks and around lips that held a smear of carmine color. He moaned and weakly fluttered eyelids suddenly too heavy to hold up.

"M-Missy . . . they . . . done for me . . . right proper," the gray-haired former mountain man panted out. "I . . . I ain't got . . . much time left."

"That's not so. We'll get you out of here to a doctor. You'll be all right," Rebecca lied, wishing it were true.

Clement Salters rolled his head from side to side, denying it. "I been shot . . . gouged . . . stabbed an' . . . cut enough . . . times to know . . . better. Don't . . . try to . . . fool a fooler. I'm . . . I'm only sorry we . . . we didn't free . . . them Appaloosies."

"We will, Salty. We will," Rebecca promised. Tears welled in her eyes, held back by a strong effort of will.

"Good . . . gal." Salty's eyes rolled up and his mouth went slack. The painful heaving of his chest ceased and he lay still, save for the tremors in his hands and feet as

182

his soul departed for greener hills.

Tenderly, Rebecca clasped the aged hulk to her bosom and wept openly.

Red Ashton looked around at the remainder of his force. He had only nine men left. Red gnawed at his lower lip, mind churning to come up with some tactic that would insure they survived and the enemy in the rocks did not. Anxious faces turned his way, masked with unspoken inquiry.

"We can't pull that one again. They'll be lookin' for it," Red said at last. "But we can make it hot for them. You two go off to the right. You an' Larrow to the left. Open up on them from the flanks. When you do, we'll move in. There's only three of 'em."

"Might be only two," one of those who had accompanied Clem Dye spoke up. "I put a shot into the old man before they got a chance to shoot back."

"Good. That makes things easier. We'll keep 'em occupied for now. You four move out."

The solid recoil of his rifle felt good to Red as he blasted away at the hillside. Bullets screamed off the rounded surfaces and howled again as the ricochets struck other boulders. Return fire seemed slack compared to earlier. Maybe Ormley had finished off the old man after all. He paused to reload as shots blasted from both flanks. Good. The boys were in position.

"Now!" he shouted as he shoved the last round into the loading gate.

Men sprang up around him and raced from the sparse cover of the trees. Red fired from the hip and his men yelled defiance as they rushed through the waving grass of the meadow. Twice he saw the weaving form of a man's broad shoulders and the yellow-orange bloom of flame from the rifle pointed in his direction. Gotta watch for that one, Red cautioned himself. He's gonna make a mistake sooner or later.

A moment later, he did.

Red squeezed off a round and grinned widely in satisfaction as the man fell back against a boulder and slowly slid to the ground.

"Yeeeeeaaaahoooo!" Yelling in triumph, Red dashed in among the rocks.

When the six outlaws charged their position, Rebecca and Thad found the situation far graver than before. Flanking fire restricted their movement and they could only pop up and trade shots at irregular intervals. It allowed the bandits to move in close without any losses. Thad jumped into an open space between two large boulders that covered his sides. He took quick aim and let go a round.

Hot lead burned into the stomach of a bowlegged gunhawk who wailed in pain as he fell to the ground. His companions left him writhing on the blood-slicked grass and pushed on toward the rocks. Rebecca came up over the top of a low rock and shot the heart out of another hard case. He flipped backward and landed within five feet of the one Thad had accounted for. Moaning slugs pelted into the spaces they occupied. She and Thad jumped back out of danger. That allowed Roger's gunmen to get within thirty feet of the hillside.

Thad appeared again and a redheaded outlaw snapped off a shot that slammed into the left side of his chest. He flew backward and bounced off a boulder behind where he had stood. Groggy, bleeding profusely, he crawled weakly away from the exposed position. Rebecca looked around, only to find the muzzles of enemy weapons closing in from every angle. All was lost.

Perhaps not so, a flash of her indomitable will dictated.

"Thad," she called in a whisper. "Lay still. Play dead and we may yet find a way out of here."

A moment later a wild rebel yell split the air and the outlaws surged into the rocks. Rebecca shot one man an inch above his belt buckle and dumped him into the rocks. His corpse fell over Thad's prostrate form. Then a rough hand grabbed her wrist and yanked the weapon from her grasp. She turned slightly and looked into the jubilant face of Red Ashton. With a sinking heart, Rebecca accepted the fact that she had become a prisoner.

Chapter 20

Throughout the entire day, Lt. Primus Clark suffered the indignity of captivity. Of far greater importance to the defeated officer was the humiliation from the loss of his command. Smarting from his scathing self-criticism, he likewise ached in every muscle of his back and legs. His feet had become swollen, blistered, and excruciatingly painful. No less, the sullen, accusing looks of his men gave him scant comfort. Worse, the Nez Percé appeared to be enjoying his degradation immensely.

They smirked at him. Or at least, that's how he saw it. Clark had been forced to walk. The mounted pair who guarded him poked him in the back with the blunt ends of their lances when he faltered. They spoke harshly in their heathen tongue and laughed in his face. Not once had he been offered water. His men had received refreshment whenever they asked for it. At last, with the sun lowering over the mountain range to the west, the caravan stopped for the night.

A potbellied Nez Percé came to where Clark stood, head hung, panting, his body afire with agony. Deftly the warrior cut the bonds that secured the lieutenant's arms. First time, Primus Clark noted, since his ignominious

apture. Well, his racing thoughts built, he'd make them
ay yet. He'd show these savages. A crafty glint came to
is eyes as he studied his captors.

Yes. That one there, Clark thought urgently. The
melly animal had *his* service revolver tucked into the
aist of his breechcloth. If he could only work his way
loser. Careful, he cautioned himself. Make it look
asual.

Clark crossed the intervening twenty feet and asked
or water. Like a mime in a dumb show, he was compelled
o act out his request. The fat Indian grunted and
odded.

"You want water?" he growled in accented English,
hile he reached for a stoppered gourd.

"Goddamn you, you speak as good of English as I do,"
he defeated lieutenant snarled. "How dare you . . . no-
o . . . I, ah, that's all right. We can all appreciate a little
oke," Clark ended as the portly Nez Percé moved to put
ack the unopened canteen. "I . . . I thank you for the
vater."

Clark gulped and slobbered, taking in long swallows in
greedy rush. His stomach cramped and he bent double,
vincing at the new pain that assailed him. When the ache
ubsided, he sucked down another long draught.

"Not good," the fat Indian with his gun cautioned.
"Make you sick."

"I . . . I'll be all right. Thirsty." All the while, Primus
Clark studied the position of the smooth walnut grips of
is .45 Colt. Just another foot closer, he gauged. Easy.
low.

Now!

Lt. Primus Clark's left hand darted outward and his
ingers closed over the plow handle grip. Before the Nez

187

Percé warrior could react, the blue-clad officer yanke
the barrel free and hooked the web of his thumb over th
hammer. Immediately the stoutly built brave slappe
Clark's gun hand out of line with his stomach and swun
an openhanded blow at the side of the officer's head.

Staggered sideways by the impact, the smack sti
ringing in his ears, Primus Clark reacted with a kick t
the Nez Percé's groin. A painful squeal ripped from th
Indian's throat as Clark's boot toe connected with h
testicles. Shouts of alarm went up from the warriors clos
by. Swiftly the Nez Percé closed in. Three of the
number raised captured rifles and eared back th
hammers. Chief Joseph thrust his way through th
gathering ring of warriors and pushed down the neares
ready muzzle.

"No," he commanded sternly.

An angry mutter rose from the scowling braves.

Wild-eyed and desperate, Clark brandished the revo
ver as he slowly turned a full circle. Everywhere he sa
the tightly drawn faces of his enemy. Shoulder t
shoulder, the Nez Percé hemmed him in. Weapons at th
ready, they tensed, poised to strike. Driven beyond th
periphery of reason by his defeat and humiliation, no
goaded by yet another failure, Clark uttered a wea
whimper and revolved within the circle once more. Hi
lips moved as he counted Indians. He raised th
revolver . . . and lowered it. Raised it . . . lowered. H
shoulders hunched, like those of a child being punishe

At last, he looked at the .45 Colt as though seeing it fo
the first time. With a soulful sob of hopelessness, Firs
Lt. Primus Clark, U. S. Army, slowly raised the handgu
and placed the muzzle between his lips.

Before Chief Joseph could leap forward to prevent i

Primus Clark yanked desperately on the trigger and blew out his brains.

"Well . . ." Red Ashton drawled as he sized up the aftermath of battle. "Your friends are all cold as stone."

A lewd grin lighted his features as he groped at his crotch. "Now you, though, I don't reckon to be all that cold a piece. 'Pears as how I got me a prime opportunity to sample some of the wares before I finish you off and take yer head to Roger Styles."

"Men have tried that before. Most of them are dead now," Rebecca answered him icily.

"Right down unflappable bitch, ain'tcha? Well, I got a little lead in my pencil that oughtta take some of the starch outta your backbone. Get outta that dress, honey, so's I can enjoy this right proper."

"Go to hell, you son of a bitch," Rebecca snarled. With the words still on her lips, her hand eased toward the beaded pouch at her waist.

Red Ashton and his surviving men had disarmed her, ignorant of the .38 Baby Russian she carried concealed in the squaw bag. Her advantage seemed limited, though, as she studied the lust-filled men surrounding her. No one held her, so she sidled to the left as Red undid his cartridge belt and the circular brass buckle beneath. He dropped his trousers, exposing himself.

But Rebecca was one step ahead of him. She moved so that Red's back now brushed the boulder she had been standing against. With the agility of a pouncing cougar, he took a bounding step toward her.

In mid-stride, his expression changed from unbounded lust to stark horror. His mouth sagged and his rigid maleness went flaccid. He worked his mouth in a soundless plea, raising one hand as though to fend off some impending danger. Then two arrows sprouted in the center of his chest.

Chilling yelps filled the confined space among the boulders. Dark figures appeared, snarling faces painted for war. More hoots and war cries sent terror into the handful of outlaws surrounding their dying leader and the supposedly helpless young woman. Red Ashton sagged to his knees, groaning, one hand clasped around the shaft of a Nez Percé arrow. Its bone and shell tip protruded from under his left shoulder blade, dripping gore. Instantly, Rebecca ducked low and dipped her hand into the squaw pouch.

She came out with the .38 Smith and Wesson cocked and ready. Knees bent slightly, both arms extended to support the small revolver, she took quick, steady aim at the nearest outlaw. The hammer fell and a dark, wet hole appeared half an inch in front of the gunhawk's left ear.

His eyes bulged and he pitched forward to sprawl over a boulder. Rebecca swung onto a new target, cocked her Baby Russian, and fired again.

Fiery lead traced a burning path through the intestines of a bowlegged rustler. He shrieked like a frightened woman and threw his hands in the air.

"Don't shoot me again! Please. I give up."

The bullet cracked over Rebecca's head and blew off the left side of his face. A quick glance up revealed Lone Wolf standing spread-legged atop a huge boulder.

"Heard the party start up and decided to join in. Thought you might like that," the tall, blond-white warrior said laconically.

Taking his sudden appearance in stride, she gave him a

cheerful wave and went back to her primary business.

Two more slugs quickly left the small Smith and Wesson she gripped and the lives of a pair of hard cases ceased in the flickering of moments.

One took the bullet in his breastbone. It shattered his sternum and sent shards of porous bone flying into his lungs. One large fragment pierced his aorta and he bled to death while attempting to raise his six-gun and kill the woman who had finished him.

While the last of his life convulsed out of him, Rebecca's other slug gouged a deep trough in the face of another of her captors. It ended its journey by removing the outlaw's nose. Howling in pain, he tried to run away, only to impale himself on a war lance in the hands of *Wahlitits*.

For a moment Rebecca could not believe that the pugnacious *Cho-pun-nish* war leader had actually come along with Lone Wolf's relief force. She couldn't doubt her senses, though, when he waved to her, grinning with the fever of blood-lust. She turned away in order to kill the last of her captors.

Rebecca shot him once in the belly. He howled and dropped to his knees, while Rebecca laid aside the Smith and took up Thad's somewhat unwieldly .45 Colt. By then the gunman had overcome his momentary paralysis of shock and raised his own revolver. Rebecca shot him again, the fatter second bullet striking his swollen abdomen only a fraction of an inch lower than the first.

The figure eight entry wounds bled hardly at all. His eyes crossed and he groaned as he sat against a blood-splattered boulder. Wonderingly, he called out in a feeble voice.

"Momma? Momma, is that you? I've got a bellyache,

191

Momma." Then he sighed out the last of his life and slid sideways into a pile of small rocks.

"That's all of them," Lone Wolf told her cheerfully a moment later.

"Oh, Thad. He's been badly wounded. Over there," she directed.

Two of the Nez Percé warriors hurried in the direction she pointed. They sorted through fallen outlaws and came up at last with a grinning Thad Walsh.

"I'm too weak to stand," he admitted. "But I fooled them into believing I was dead." Then he lapsed into Shahaptian and repeated it for the warriors.

"We'll get you to a doctor soon, Thad," Rebecca promised.

"And we'd better get to Pendleton fast," Lone Wolf added. "*Wahlitits* came along on this only for a chance to kill whites. Shame if we don't turn him loose on Roger and what's left of the gang."

All three of the street lamps in Pendleton, Oregon had been extinguished by the time Rebecca, Lone Wolf, and four Nez Percé warriors, led by *Wahlitits*, entered the deserted streets. Weapons at the ready, they walked their horses along the main thoroughfare, alert for any indication of trouble.

"Your men will be in position at the corrals?" Rebecca asked *Wahlitits* in Lakota, while repeating the question in sign language.

"Yes," the squat, powerful warrior replied in a grunt. "We kill all whites here?"

"No," Rebecca snapped. "Not all of them had anything to do with stealing your horses or killing anyone."

"They are white," *Wahlitits* answered simply.

A block farther on, four dark forms emerged from the deeper blackness of shadow. "Hold it right there."

Three of Roger's men and the sheriff stood in the middle of the street. The rustlers held their six-guns casually. Sheriff Holman gripped the forestock of a sawed-off Parker twelve gauge. The twin muzzles pointed directly at Rebecca's chest.

"You're one of the people we've come to see, Sheriff," Rebecca told him with disarming mildness.

"Throw down your weapons. You're all under arrest."

"What for, Sheriff? Disturbing the peace? Vagrancy? Loitering?" A teasing tone had entered Rebecca's voice.

"Try starting with murder, assault with intent to commit murder, mayhem."

"Ah! 'Mayhem.' One of Roger Styles's favorite words. He used it on a false 'wanted' poster one time."

"Drop that horse pistol, Sister, or I'll cut you in half with this scatter-gun," the sheriff menaced.

"I'll put it in the holster, but I'll not drop it."

"Do it, then. The rest of you, give up your arms."

Rebecca complied wordlessly. Once her .44 Smith American rested in the thick saddle holster, she reached casually to her beaded pouch. The sheriff relaxed his guard slightly as the Nez Percé warriors lowered their bows and made to drop them on the ground.

This was going to be easy, Hezekiah Holman gloated. Roger had told him how dangerous this woman was. Ha! Roger had to be a weakling to believe that. All he had to do now was blow her head off. Holman took a step forward.

Rebecca shot him in the white space between his thick, grinning lips.

Her bullet blasted out the bottom of her squaw pouch.

Smoking bits of elkhide and a shower of colored beads slashed into the sheriff's face before the hot slug shattered teeth and tore through the back of Holman's mouth. Hezekiah Holman rocked back on his heels and his shotgun discharged skyward. Recoil sent him toward the ground—dead.

Before he hit, Lone Wolf swung up his long-barreled Remington revolver and put a .44 bullet into the breastbone of the nearest of Roger Styles's gunhawks. Spitting blood, the outlaw spun to one side and stumbled into the path of his sidekick.

His aim spoiled by the collision, the hard case managed only a single shot, which creased the skin on *Wahlitits*'s left shoulder, before a Nez Percé warrior buried a tomahawk in the top of his skull. The other members of the improvised posse scattered. Rebecca elevated her aim slightly and again fired from inside her pouch.

Blood flew from the meaty portion of a rustler's shoulder where his neck joined. The bullet from Rebecca's .38 Smith had cut a vital artery and a scarlet geyser sprayed up beside his right ear. From down the street, a rifle barked through the side window of the Pendleton Livestock Company.

"Someone's in Roger's office," Rebecca yelled.

"We'll flush him out soon enough," Lone Wolf assured her.

"My men will go after those," *Wahlitits* signed, indicating the fleeing hard cases.

"Good. Look after your wound," Rebecca advised.

"It is nothing," the stalwart Nez Percé replied.

"Fix it anyhow," Rebecca ordered sharply.

"Women. They are all alike," *Wahlitits* complained in

Shahaptian. "They want to boss a man around." Laughing, he drew a length of cloth from his war bag and began to bind the wound.

Jason Brill trembled slightly as he worked the lever action of the Winchester that Roger Styles had given him. He knelt at the side window of Roger's office. It was a part of Roger's plan to eliminate the Caldwell girl in the event she and anyone with her got past the ambush outside town. Even so, it didn't make a lot of sense to Jason. What was *he* doing in *Roger*'s office? And why had Roger chosen to take up a position in the hotel, opposite the bank? Shouldn't he, as banker, be closest to his own interests? He watched the dark figures down the street spread apart and go about their separate tasks. Two came his way, on opposite sides of the street. He put the rifle to his shoulder and sighted on the slighter built of the pair.

"Balderdash!" Jason muttered aloud.

He had squeezed the trigger a moment after the target disappeared into the darkness of an alleyway between two buildings. Smoke still obscured his view. Not a fragment of breeze stirred through the sleeping hamlet. When Jason could see again, both of his intended victims had gotten out of sight. A moment later, the night lit up with bright orange flashes.

Window panes shattered, showering him with shards of glass. Bullets punched through the thin walls of the building and moaned past his head and body. Jason dropped the rifle, curled into a ball, arms wrapped around his head for protection, and moaned in terror. They really *were* coming after him.

Made frantic by the thought, Jason snatched up the

Winchester and crawled toward the door. His quaking fingers fumbled for the knob and eased it free. Cautiously, he opened the thin portal a crack and peered out.

All he could see was horses. Hundreds of spotted-rump ponies, milling in the corral. Damn those animals and double-damn the man who got him involved with them. Silently and bitterly, he cursed the strangers who sought to harm him, Roger Styles, and the Nez Percé. Gathering the fleeing shards of his dubious courage, Jason opened the door wider. After a deep breath, he exposed his head and hazarded a quick look to right and left.

No one. He could see no threat, actual or implied. Only darkness and those damned horses. Jason drew a deep, shaky breath. He hadn't heard any shots from the hotel. What was Roger doing? Why had he not backed Sheriff Holman and finished it right there? Enough doubts and enough taking of risks.

The way lay clear for him to escape through the back streets to the safety of his home. No one would ever know of his involvement. At least nothing that could be proven. Let Roger Styles fight his own battles. *He* wasn't about to stay around and be a target for someone who could down two men with a revolver hidden behind the smoldering bottom of an Indian pouch. Not Jason Brill.

Brill rose on trembly legs and swung the portal wide. Another quick glance to both sides, then he slipped out into the night. He reached the corral rails in four fast, shuffling strides. Away from his vulnerable position now, Jason breathed a bit more easily. He took two sidling steps along the stock pens, then froze.

Had he seen the shape of a person off to the right?

Gulping back his fear, Brill took another step.

"That's far enough," a feminine voice demanded.

A woman? Hell, he could handle that any time. Emboldened, Brill took another pace forward and brought his rifle up to his hip, so that it aimed toward the woman.

"Take another step and I'll blow your head off," a male voice growled from behind him.

Trapped!

Terror seized Jason Brill. Like a rat in a burning building, he could only think of going upward to escape his doom. He let go of the Winchester and started to climb.

Fright added speed to his movements. He reached the top rail before Rebecca Caldwell could take a bead on the corrupt banker. She aimed to disable him, placing her sights on the meaty portion of one thing. Gently she squeezed the trigger.

Flame bloomed and smoke billowed. Through the reverberation of her gunshot, Rebecca heard a pained yelp from Jason Brill. A heavy thump indicated he had fallen to the ground.

Then came a horror-filled scream that sent Rebecca running forward to where the banker had disappeared off the top rail. Jason Brill lay in a spreading pool of his blood. Eyes wide and white with terror, he looked at the milling horses that walked all around him. A low groan came from deep in his chest. From different points within the complex of corrals came the distinct sound of gates being opened. Brill raised his arms in helpless supplication.

"P-please. Get me out of her. *Please!*"

"Can you stand?" Rebecca asked him.

"N-no. You shot me in the leg and . . . I twisted the other ankle when I fell. Please, you've got to help me."

Another gate creaked open, the large main one, Rebecca observed. "I'm afraid it's too late."

"Noooooooooo!" Jason Brill howled as shouts came from the various pens and the purloined Palouse horses bolted into frenetic running.

His bellow of stark terror changed to a thin, high wail, which vanished shortly under the pounding hoofs of the Nez Percé spotted-rump ponies.

In only moments, his overstuffed bulk became reduced to a wide, muddy splash of broken bones, blood, and ruin.

When the sound of drumming hoofs diminished enough for conversation, Rebecca turned to Lone Wolf. "Now we have to find Roger Styles."

Chapter 21

"Roger has that little house at the edge of town," Lone Wolf remarked.

"I don't think he'll be there. Let's try the hotel first."

"Why?"

"Roger had a nice little trap set for us, right? The ambush outside town. Then, if that failed, the sheriff and three men waiting for us. And the banker, Brill, in Roger's office. Why not Roger? The answer seems obvious.

"Roger wanted an overview of what went on. So, I think he would have been in the hotel."

Lone Wolf nodded to acknowledge her logic and started toward the tall building a block and a half away. At the first intersection, two thoroughly demoralized outlaws charged them on horseback. Six-guns blazed in the night. Wild bullets forced Rebecca and Lone Wolf to leap apart.

One slug shattered the glass globe atop a lamp post. A shower of razor-edged bits flew around them. Another split the air with a wicked crack beside Rebecca's head. She swung up her .44 Smith and Wesson and returned fire.

A howl of sheer pain cut off in the middle to a

mournful moan as Rebecca's bullet smashed into his lower stomach. Its erratic course left behind a gory trail of destruction as it shattered his left kidney. Then he folded forward and draped his lifeless body over the animal's neck. His partner fared not a bit better.

"How many more can there be?" Lone Wolf asked, panting.

"I don't want to make a guess."

"Let's hope the rest are guarding Roger's house."

Loud whoops came from the far end of town. Several shots split the quiet of midnight and a man screamed as though in mortal terror. More war cries sounded and the skyline began to glow redly.

"*Wahlitits* and his men have set Roger's place on fire."

"That should keep the survivors too busy to come after us," Rebecca agreed.

Lone Wolf motioned toward the hotel. "Now's the time to hit Roger before he makes a break for it."

No other shots interrupted their short journey. The hotel door, though closed, was unlocked. Crouching low, Rebecca and Lone Wolf entered the lobby.

Only silence greeted them.

In the dim light from outside, Rebecca motioned to the stairway. Lone Wolf nodded and indicated he would take the back way. On silent feet, they headed for the second floor. No shots blazed down the front stairwell by the time Rebecca reached the landing. Equal quiet came from the rear of the building. In a rush, she negotiated the second flight.

Still all pervading stillness.

Rebecca saw movement at the far end of the hall. She tensed, ready to fire the big .44 Smith and Wesson in her right fist. Then she recognized Lone Wolf. They met in the center of the hall. On tiptoe, they went to the doorway that gave access to the balcony. It hung ajar. Without spoken instructions, each did the necessary, standing to the sides. Then Lone Wolf dived through and came up in a crouch.

Nobody there. His highly tuned senses could almost feel the recent presence of someone. Now only emptiness mocked his efforts. He rose and stepped back inside the hotel's second floor. A negative shake of his head confirmed what Rebecca expected to learn. She pointed to a doorway.

Together they began to try the rooms that had windows overlooking the street.

The first one was locked and still. Lone Wolf produced a skeleton key and inserted it in the cast-iron lock. The tumblers turned noisily and he jumped away, fearful of bullets through the panels. A long moment went by and he reached out gingerly to turn the knob. The door swung open on nothingness.

Empty. They tried another.

Hinges squeaked as the thin portal swung inward. Another blank, they realized a moment after Lone Wolf dived onto the threadbare carpet, doing a roll and up to make a fast cast of the room. Only two left.

Behind the next door, Rebecca's keen hearing detected creaking and rustling sounds. A groan came through clearly. It could be. Roger might have a hostage. She stepped back while Lone Wolf kicked in the flimsy partition.

"What th' hell!" a man's voice exploded from the bed.

"Yeeek!" a tiny female voice sounded.

"Uh . . . sorry. Wrong room," Lone Wolf stammered, averting his gaze from the naked couple.

"See here, we're on our honeymoon. A little chivaree's one thing, but this is too much."

"Sorry. It's all a mistake," Rebecca added to her companion's earlier apology. She looked sympathetically at the girl.

Honeymoon, she thought. Why, she's hardly more than a child. Couldn't be over fourteen. A wedding band sparkled on the third finger of the youthful bride's left hand, illuminated by the low light of a kerosene lamp. Shattered composure wrapped around them, Rebecca and Lone Wolf tried to make a tactful retreat. One room left.

Another locked door. It yielded readily to Lone Wolf's skeleton key. No Roger, however. No one at all. Discouraged, Rebecca walked to the window. A muffled boom came from across the street. Rebecca looked that way quickly enough to see the dying glow from the explosion. Dust billowed around the foundation of the bank, roiled up by the ground shock.

Acrid smoke filled the bank. Roger Styles choked on it as he wrenched open the flimsy door to the vault with a crowbar. He stumbled on fallen safety deposit boxes and entered hurriedly. He scratched up light with a lucifer, its sulphurous stench unnoticed in the odor of burned dynamite, and located a kerosene lamp. The blast had broken the globe, but the nickel-plated base remained unharmed. He touched his match to the wick and turned it up to the edge of smoking. His eyes glowed with a sinister hunger.

There it lay. Bags of money. Much more than he had on deposit. More, even, than he could carry away. But he

ould take all he could in the little time he had. The
xplosion would be heard. No getting around that. It
ould send that nincompoop, Brill, running here from
e stock pens. So what. If Rebecca Caldwell didn't kill
e fat little slug, he'd take care of that when the banker
rived to find his hoard looted.

Swiftly Roger set to work.

He opened one bag and began stuffing sheaves of large
enomination bills into an oversized carpet bag. "Care-
l," he cautioned himself aloud. "Make it neat. You can
ke a lot more that way."

Suddenly he laughed aloud. "Oh, my. Oh, my, my, my.
oger Styles, criminal mastermind, actually robbing a
ank like a common brigand. Whatever will come next?"

Roger continued to chortle to himself as he jammed
ore currency into the extra large valise.

"That's Roger," Rebecca said positively. "He's after
e money."

"We can get him from here," Lone Wolf suggested.

"Not if there's a back way out. You stay, cover the
reet. I'm going around behind the building."

Without waiting for any comment, Rebecca left the
oom hurriedly and ran to the stairway. In seconds she
merged from the hotel and crossed the street. An alley
an behind the row of business establishments along
endleton's main street. Rebecca entered it cautiously
nd hurried toward the bank.

Unnoticed in her hurry, a second-story window slid
pen partway down the narrow passageway. The dark
ilhouette of a man's head and shoulders and the long
arrel of his six-gun poked outward before the stile

reached its furthest upward position. In the last fe
inches of its movement, the raw wood of the sash bou
against the casement. It produced a loud squeal. Witho
changing pace, Rebecca swung around and whipped h
.44 Smith and Wesson upward. The head and shoulde
filled her rear sight. Instantly she squeezed the trigge

Lost in the loud report, the would-be assassin's wail
anguish followed him to the ground as he pitche
headfirst out the window. Rebecca nodded in satisfactie
and trotted on toward the bank. At half a block
distance, she saw movement at the back of the buildin

Crouched low, Roger Styles came out, bent double I
the weight of a large carpetbag bulging with neat
banded stacks of currency. He scurried in the opposi
direction, forced into a crablike gait by his burde
Rebecca recognized him at once and brought up h
Smith and Wesson. She used the web of her right hand
ratchet back the hammer.

Roger heard the telltale clicks behind him and spu
around, a nickel-plated Colt .45 in his left hand. He fire
first.

The bullet smacked solidly into the clapboard rear wa
of the general mercantile. Sprays of slivers assaile
Rebecca's face. Sharp pinpoints of pain radiated from he
left cheek. Her eyes stung and she feared she might ha
been blinded in one eye. The combined effect of physic
damage and pressing danger put her aim off.

The .44 slug passed a foot over Roger's head. He fire
again and began to run. Rebecca pounded after him. I
panic now, Roger fired over his shoulder. Yellow-orang
light brightened the alley. The bullet gouged flesh fro
the point of Rebecca's right shoulder.

Numbed, her fingers released the Smith and Wesso

It landed with a thud. Roger showed a flash of white teeth behind a grim smile as he raised his revolver for a final, deadly shot.

With uncalculated speed, his target disappeared.

Rebecca leaped aside, into the recessed entryway of the mercantile. She hugged the door panel and fought to still her breath. Any moment, she expected Roger to figure out what she had done and come for her. She had to remain in place, until Roger got close enough for her to use her skinning knife. Left-handed she hadn't the strength normal for her, but she figured she could cut him deeply enough to end the danger to herself.

Thirty seconds passed. Counting heartbeats, Rebecca remained motionless in the doorway. A minute dragged by. Where was Roger? How close now? Her mind jumbled with urgent questions. Still no indication of what he was doing. Not even a crunching footstep on the alley floor.

Another minute. She could endure this fatal inactivity no longer. Rebecca leaned forward and peered into the alley.

No sign of Roger Styles. He had gone away as though he had never existed. Ears straining for some clue, Rebecca heard the distant rumble of hoofbeats. Someone was galloping a horse out of town.

That someone, she knew with a sinking sense of defeat, had to be Roger Styles.

"I still want to buy some of your spotted-rump horses," Rebecca declared three days later at the Clearwater village of Looking Glass. Her wound in the shoulder still burned and stung, though it had been carefully cleaned and bandaged. It caused her to move stiffly.

"Two of them," she went on. "And Lone Wolf wants one."

"No. You not buy them," Fall Buffalo said, implacable.

"Why . . . why not?" Rebecca could not understand this reticence. "We will trade then?"

"No. No trade."

"I'll only go elsewhere," she revealed, her jaw firm in determination.

"There is no need for that," Looking Glass informed her. "You have done much for our people. You have kept the peace," he began to enumerate. "You have recovered our horses. The army has come to assure us there will be no more men like the sun-touched soldier chief who took his own life. None of this could have been done without you."

"Then why can't I buy or trade for some Palouse horses?"

A broad smile blossomed on Looking Glass's face. "The spotted-rumps are yours. You may chose any three for yourself. Two for the *Absaroka* warrior, Lone Wolf. A gift from my people to you. We are proud to have known you. Take the best our herds have to offer. Ride them like the wind. We will always be grateful. You are a mighty warrior, *Šinaskawin* of the Dakota."

Astounded, Rebecca stammered a reply. "I . . . I . . . I'm overwhelmed. This is a gift beyond any I could imagine. Oh, thank you, Looking Glass. Thank you all," she added, throwing wide her arms as though to embrace all the *Cho-pun-nish*.

"Where do you go now, *Šinaskawin?*" Looking Glass

206

inquired politely.

"South, I think. And west to California. Roger Styles rode that way and I intend to find him."

"There will always be whites like Roger Styles," *Wahlitits* complained.

"Yes. That's true enough, *Wahlitits*," Rebecca replied through the translator. "And I'll fight them, as well as Roger, whenever I encounter them."

"It is too little. Even a mighty warrior woman like *Sinaskawin* cannot scoop up all the grains of sand along the Snake River. The day will come when these bad ones will win out over our people. Some day there will be war between the whites and the *Cho-pun-nish*. A war that will not be of our making," he added.

Rebecca smiled at this acknowledgement that *Wahlitits* would not take the warpath against the white settlers of Oregon. "You are wise and brave, *Wahlitits*. I only hope you are not so good at telling the future. Now, let's select those horses. I'm looking forward to gaining their confidence, riding them today, then the feast."

"Tomorrow you start for the big water in the south?" Looking Glass inquired.

"No. Not right away." Heat blossomed in Rebecca's lithe body as she thought of the power in Thad Walsh's manly loins. Her wound would leave a scar. She wondered idly if Thad would still find her attractive with a puckered dent in the point of her shoulder. Yes. It would make no difference. He'd seen the other white cicatrice lines, souvenirs of her long campaign against Roger Styles, Jake Tulley, and her cursed uncles. Would she ever see Ezekial Caldwell again? Or Roger Styles? Enough of that, though, she firmly told herself. Back to the business at hand.

"I have to stop off and visit Thad Walsh. Without him, none of this could have been done."

"It is good for you to see him," Looking Glass advised, a knowing twinkle in his eyes.

"And to love him again," Rebecca thought silently. Oh, yes. *To love him a whole lot.*

Then . . .

Then, on to California.